Out of
Bounds

Out of Bounds

Andrea Montalbano

sourcebooks
jabberwocky

Published by Sourcebooks Jabberwocky, an imprint of Sourcebooks, Inc.
P.O. Box 4410, Naperville, Illinois 60567-4410
(630) 961-3900
Fax: (630) 961-2168
www.sourcebooks.com

Library of Congress Cataloging-in-Publication Data

Names: Montalbano, Andrea, author.
Title: Out of bounds / Andrea Montalbano.
Other titles: Lily out of bounds
Description: Naperville, IL : Sourcebooks Jabberwocky, [2017] | Series:
    Soccer Sisters ; [1] | Originally published: New York : In This Together
    Media, 2012 under the title Lily out of bounds. | Summary: When newcomer
    Skylar joins the Brookville Breakers soccer team, Makena James ignores the
    Soccer Sisters code--and family rules--to try to win Skylar's approval.
Identifiers: LCCN 2016030784 | (13 : alk. paper)
Subjects: | CYAC: Soccer--Fiction. | Teamwork (Sports)--Fiction. | Family
    life--Fiction.
Classification: LCC PZ7.M76342 Out 2017 | DDC [Fic]--dc23 LC record
available at https://lccn.loc.gov/2016030784

Source of Production: Versa Press, East Peoria, Illinois, USA
Date of Production: February 2017
Run Number: 5008495

Printed and bound in the United States of America.
VP 10 9 8 7 6 5 4 3 2 1

This series is dedicated to Soccer Sisters everywhere.

1

Makena Walsh inhaled the smell of the sweet spring grass as a gentle breeze tickled her face and a drop of sweat rolled down her neck. Soccer was an awesome and simple game, and there was nothing in the world she loved more than being outside, playing with friends, kicking, and running free.

But, as much as Makena loved playing soccer, she hated losing. And right now, all she could think about was the fact that her team was about to lose the league championship. Slowly, she released her breath with a loud sigh. A sigh that ended up sounding a lot more like a groan.

A sharp voice jolted her back to reality.

"Hey, Mac, thanks for the commentary. How about listening to me tell you how you and your teammates are going to turn this game around?"

Makena looked up to see Coach Lily and every one of her teammates staring at her as they sat in the halftime huddle. A few of her friends started to chuckle.

"Sorry, Coach. I am listening," she muttered lamely, grabbing her water bottle.

"Good," her coach answered, with just a hint of a smile. "Now listen up. For the second half, we'll start like this: Val, up front. Makena, you stay in the midfield. Chloe, on the outside. And, Jessie, you'll drop back to right back. Everyone else stays the same. Got it?"

There was a murmur of agreement from the team as they all got to their feet. They started to shuffle back to the field, but Makena had a pit in her stomach.

Her best friend, Val Flores, walked up beside her.

"Well, here we go again," she said as the two girls walked side by side.

Makena responded, "I *cannot believe* we are losing to…"

"The Leewood Lions… Roar, roar, roar." Val finished her sentence with a mock cheer. Makena smiled. Even in her most dire moments, Val could find a way to make her laugh.

"What is it with this team? Every time we play them, we fall apart," Makena said. "I just don't get it."

Val stopped to adjust her shin guard and retie her cleats as Makena surveyed the other team across the field. The Lions wore red-and-black-striped uniforms and were taking their positions on the other side of the pitch. Several of them were bouncing on their toes, and Makena thought they looked pretty smug.

"Well, they certainly don't give up," Val said. This was the third time they had faced the Lions, and in every previous match, the Breakers had given up a lead to lose or tie. So far, today was no different. After scoring an early easy goal, they were now losing 2 to 1.

We've got to find a way to turn this around, Makena thought.

"Well, here we go," Jessie said, jogging up from behind, "Danger vu all over again."

Val looked up at Jessie, squinting through the afternoon sun with a puzzled look.

"Danger what now?" Makena asked. "Jessie, what the heck is danger vu?"

"You know, when you've seen something before that's kind of scary and it's happening again. *Danger vu.*"

Makena just shook her head, smiling. Typical Jessie. If Val was the one friend who could make Makena laugh in a crisis, Jessie was her one buddy certain to say something dopey. *Good thing she's such a good defender*, Makena thought to herself.

Val rolled her eyes, stood up, and laughed, "Déjà vu. Déjà vuuuuu."

"Whatev," Jessie said. "All I know is we are losing to this stupid team again."

Losing was not something Makena's team, the Brookville Breakers, was used to. As one of the top travel teams in their state, the Breakers had had an undefeated season so far. Well, that is, not counting the loss and tie to Leewood in the fall.

"They aren't even that good," Makena muttered.

"Yeah, but they are dirty," Val said. Makena nodded in agreement, rubbing her thigh where their center forward had kneed her early in the game.

"Look alive, ladies!" a voice boomed from the sidelines. Makena turned to see Coach Lily pacing near the bench on the sideline after giving some last-minute advice to Chloe Gordon, one of their forwards. Chloe sprinted out to the group, looking as graceful as ever.

"Oh man," she said as she reached them. "I've never seen Coach so stressed out before."

"Really?" Makena peered to the sideline. Coach Lily was intense but usually pretty calm.

It was time to start, but Makena felt like someone or something else was missing. She looked around at her team. They were all here: Val, Chloe, Jessie, Ariana, Sydney, Kat, Harper, Tessa, Jasmine, Ella, and Abby.

Suddenly, it hit her. The Breakers had forgotten to do their halftime cheer.

"Guys! Bring it in! Quick!" she called. Makena was like most soccer players: very superstitious. Not doing their cheer would definitely seal their fate.

All the Breakers sprinted to form a circle. Every girl put a hand into the center.

"We can do this," Makena said. "We can't give up."

"You know that's what Coach just told me, right?" Chloe asked with a grin.

Ariana, the goalie, stood up tall to mimic, "You have to give one hundred percent effort one hundred percent of the time, girls. And not just for thirty minutes…" She paused, and the rest of the team joined in, "For thirty-one minutes!"

Makena and the rest of the girls laughed. They all knew Coach Lily's sayings by heart. Sometimes they even spilled into Makena's dreams: Win every ball. Play until the whistle blows. Leave it on the field.

"Coach is right," Val chimed in with a serious voice.

"We can't give up and let these guys beat us again. We are better."

The referee blew his whistle to signal the girls to take their places and start the second half. The Lions were in position, and everyone was waiting. But the Breakers ignored the referee and lingered in their circle a moment longer.

"We've got this, Breakers," Makena said to her friends and teammates. "We can do this. But we have to do it together."

"Team!" Val echoed.

"OK, Breakers on three," Makena said, searching for the fire in the eyes of her teammates. Makena looked at Ariana. She saw the spark in the goalie's eyes. She saw the determination on Val's face. The sick feeling began to turn to butterflies of excitement. She started to believe maybe they could…no, they *would* do this.

Makena inhaled and yelled in her loudest voice, "One, two, three!"

Her teammates answered her call. In one voice they yelled, "BREAKERS!"

It was the Breakers' turn to kick off. Chloe and Val immediately attacked down the middle. Val got open and dribbled forward into space. She went to shoot, but a Lion defender tackled her hard. Val tumbled to the ground, and the referee whistled for a foul.

"Are you out of your mind?" a parent yelled from the sideline. "You need glasses, ref! That little butterfly took a dive."

Makena glared at the man. Val would never take a dive. She was small for her age but as tough as they came. Makena recognized a father from the other team. He'd been to all their games, and just like last time, his face was red with anger and his arms raised and flexed. Why do some parents think that yelling at the ref helps their children in any way? It was just embarrassing for everyone.

Chloe raced over to help Val up. "You OK?"

"I'm good," Val said, peering to the sidelines. "Oh, I see Musclehead is back. Let's beat these guys."

Val restarted the ball quickly, but the Lions were ready to pounce, sending a long, looping pass over the top of the Breakers' defense. Jessie was caught off guard, and the Lion striker, a tall, dark-haired girl with amazing speed, took off down the line. If she cut inside, she would be one-on-one with the goalie. *Oh, no*, Makena thought. She sprinted back toward her own goal, keeping an eye on Jessie giving chase.

Makena loved the feel of her strong legs as she sprinted down the field. Jessie was able to gain some ground, but

Makena knew it was up to her to intercept any cross or pass in front of the goal. The Lion attacker got to the corner and made a beautiful turn to the inside. With her right foot, she crossed the ball into the middle of the field. It was on the ground, and that meant it was very dangerous. All it would take was a deflection to redirect it past the goalie. Not even awesome Ariana would have a chance to save it. Makena spotted an incoming player, number fourteen, making a run toward the ball.

Makena's legs burned and her chest ached, but she couldn't stop. She wouldn't.

"Get number fourteen!" Chloe yelled.

Number fourteen arrived as the ball rolled across the face of the goal. Makena had to win it but without tripping or pushing. She was so tired but willed her legs to keep going.

Time seemed to slow for Makena, and her soccer instincts took over. She jumped and reached out her foot to block the shot. It wasn't enough to stop the ball, but it was enough to pop it up into the air.

"Keeper's ball!" Ariana yelled, running forward.

But the ball was spinning and, as it hit the ground, shot to the side and slipped out of Ariana's grasp. It bounced free in front of the goal. Makena scrambled to her feet, and it was a race to see who could get to the ball first.

"Away! Away! Away!" Coach Lily yelled. "Clear the ball!"

"Shoot!" she heard the other team's sideline cry.

But Ariana recovered. She jumped at the bouncing ball and smothered it with her body. All Makena could see was her curled back with the number one on it. She sighed with relief and leaned on the goalpost to catch her breath. That was close. Way too close. She lifted her head to see all the Breakers sharing the same look of anxiety.

Everyone except Ariana.

When she finally lifted her head, Makena saw a little smirk.

Sometimes in soccer it just takes that one moment to turn things around. One amazing save or one great play or even dumb luck can change a game's momentum. In this case, it was that smirk. There was something in her look that Makena recognized: Ariana wasn't giving up.

And neither was she.

"Play on!" the referee called.

Ariana stood and gave the signal that she was going to punt. The girls on both teams backed up. Val moved all the way to half-field and waited for the ball. But Makena hung back close to Ariana, pretending to be too out of breath. As soon as both teams were far upfield, Ariana rolled the ball directly to Makena's foot. The Lions reacted by pressing forward as a team, trying to steal the ball from her. Makena took a touch, lifted her head, and saw Val making a run. She launched the ball deep up the sideline into the space. Val timed it perfectly so she didn't even have to break her stride. Before the Lions knew what had happened, Val was one-on-one against the goalie. She dribbled into the box and shot. Hard and low and right into the back of the net.

Goal!

"Yes!" Makena cried as all the Breakers ran to hug Val. Out of the corner of her eye, she saw Coach Lily raise her fist. The Breakers parents cheered, and Makena laughed when Jessie's dad tumbled out of his folding chair mid-yell.

"Way to go, Breakers!" he yelled from the ground.

It was now or never.

"OK, guys. There are only a few minutes left in the game. If we tie, they win the league. If we win, the trophy is ours. We've worked too hard to let this slip away to this team again," Makena said to her teammates. Practices three times a week all fall, tournaments all winter, and an intense spring season. This was it. All their effort and commitment was on the line.

It was Leewood's turn to restart the ball. Makena looked to the sideline to her coach. She held up her hand. Five fingers. Five minutes left. Five minutes to dig deep.

But like in all their previous matches, the Lions came back strong. Everyone knew the clock was ticking. The Breakers started working upfield. The Lions only needed a tie to win the league, so they were happy to waste time and kept kicking the ball out of bounds.

Makena felt the excitement rising.

"Come on, Breakers!" one of the parents called.

Chloe sprinted to retrieve the ball. She had to get it back in play.

"Chloe!" Val called as she made a run to the center of the box. Val got the ball at her feet. But she had to fight to keep it. She was swarmed by defenders and was being jostled by the Lions' center defender. The girl was a head taller than Val and looked like she could be in high school. Just as she went to shoot, the center defender tackled her hard. Val went flying and the whistle blew. Foul.

Makena held her breath to see if the referee would award a penalty kick.

He didn't. Instead, he picked up the ball and placed it just outside the eighteen-yard box and pointed toward the goal. Makena knew that meant that while it was a free kick, the Lion defenders were allowed to stand in front of the ball and form a wall to try to block the shot.

Makena looked to the sideline but already knew what

she would see. Her coach was holding up three fingers. The Lion players started whispering. They knew there were only a few seconds left in the game. The referee was looking at his watch. This had to be the last play of the game.

"Why is she holding up *three* fingers?" Makena heard one girl ask. Another said, "Their coach doesn't even know how much time is left."

But every one of the Breakers knew that Coach Lily knew exactly how much time was left and what she wanted them to do. Her three fingers in the air weren't how much time was left but the sign that she wanted to use play number three, the one they had been working on so much in practice.

Makena could hear her coach's voice in her head. *Keep your eye on the ball, and when you strike it, keep your head down or it will fly over the goal.* Val and Abby stood next to the ball, chatting like they were not paying attention. Makena stood back and to the right, and Chloe lined up as the kicker. She studied the wall of Lions players standing just ten yards in front of her.

The whistle blew, and Chloe moved toward the ball as if to shoot, but instead she leapt over the ball and ran toward the wall. The Lions' defense was taken by surprise. The wall froze in place, watching Chloe instead of the ball. Just then, Val tapped the ball through Jessie's legs, and it rolled to the right of the wall. It was perfect. Makena blocked out the screams and focused. She kept her head down and blasted a shot. The goalie never even moved. Makena felt the release and watched as the ball flew through the air and into the upper-right corner, slamming into the back of the net.

Goal!

The Lions were king of this jungle no more.

The girls rushed one another, colliding and falling to the ground in a heap of squealing joy. The whistle blew, and the Breakers from the sideline joined the pile on the ground hugging and laughing.

"Yes!" Makena yelled as she struggled to get to her feet. The girls put their arms around one another and began to jump up and down in celebration.

Makena looked from face to face. Each of the girls was special to her in her own way. They shared not only experiences but also a special understanding of what it means to work together. Makena thought of them as her sisters. The kind of sister you choose. The kind that picks you up and wipes you off when you get tripped. The kind who always has your back. And, the kind that finally beats Leewood.

Makena and the Breakers were connected in a way that had nothing to do with DNA but everything to do with *team*.

They were the best kind of sisters: Soccer Sisters.

2

Makena closed her eyes and savored the last delicious bite of her burger.

"That may have been the greatest burger of my life," she said with a sigh, wiping her face and sitting back in the booth.

After a game, Makena was so hungry that anything tasted great, but a burger with the works? Well, that was heaven on a plate.

The girls were crammed in a booth, upholding one of the team's most important and treasured postgame traditions: eating.

Whenever they had an away game, they begged their parents to drive them to the diner closest to the field. Diners with ten-page menus made everyone happy. This weekend, it was the usual crew: Makena, Val, Jessie, Chloe,

Ariana, Ella, and a surprise guest in the form of Coach Lily. Coach Lily was sitting with the parents at another table nearby.

"You going to finish that?" Jessie asked Makena, trying to steal her last french fry.

Makena playfully slapped her hand away. "Get your own fries. It's not my fault you ordered a salad."

Val laughed, then handed Jessie one of her own fries. "Jessie, when are you going to learn to eat real food?"

"Salad is real food," Jessie said, waving a forkful of greens.

"Not after soccer games!" Val said with a laugh.

Chloe's arm reached in like a snake and grabbed Makena's last precious fry.

"You snooze, you lose," Chloe joked.

"Hey!" Makena yelled halfheartedly.

Their waitress approached the table. "Can I clear any of this out of your way?" she asked.

"I am so stuffed," Makena said, rubbing her belly and handing her plate to the waitress with a smile. The table looked like the remnants of a battlefield.

Suddenly, Ariana shouted, "Let's get a sundae!"

"Oh yeah," Makena replied, suddenly starving again. "With six spoons please. One for each of us."

Coach Lily approached the table. She was a former college player, and Makena loved how she still moved like an athlete.

"Hey, girls. Again, great comeback today. It was good to finally keep it together against that team," Lily said. There was nothing better than praise from their coach.

"So, girls, I got the schedule for next weekend. You are not going to believe who our first opponent is."

Makena could feel her heart quicken. The girls looked at one another.

"Who?" Val asked immediately.

"Guess."

"Larchmont?"

Lily shook her head.

"World Class Strikers?"

"Nope. Westside!"

"Westside!" Val blurted out.

Makena sat back, and several of the girls groaned. The Westside Wildcats were another one of their big rivals.

"Why the heck do we travel all the way to Philadelphia to play a team from nearby?"

"It's a pretty big tournament, so all the big clubs go," Lily said.

"Can you believe this?" Makena asked Chloe.

"No, but I can't play anyway. I have a stupid recital," Chloe said.

"You aren't coming?" Makena asked. Tournaments were Makena's absolute favorite thing. She loved staying in hotel rooms with her friends, going out to eat, slumber parties. All of it.

"But without Chloe and with Harper not coming, will we even have enough players?" Val asked.

Their coach answered, "I've asked a player to join us for the summer. She'll be in Philly this weekend."

Makena's jaw dropped a little bit. A new player? New players sometimes came to the team but usually in the fall.

"You mean she's joining the team?" Ariana asked, surprised.

"Yes. For the summer and possibly for the fall season. I think she'll help us."

"Where is she from?" Val asked.

"New Jersey. She's on the New Jersey State Team as well."

Whoa, Makena thought. New Jersey had some of the strongest teams in the country. Carli Lloyd was from New Jersey! This girl must be something special.

"She sounds awesome!" Makena exclaimed, excited to get the chance to play with someone like that, but the second she saw the look on Chloe's face, Makena wished she could shove the words right back in her mouth.

"I gotta go," Coach Lily said. "See you girls later."

As she turned leave, their coach nearly knocked over the waitress, who was carrying an enormous ice cream sundae dripping with gobs of chocolate and whipped cream.

"Wow!" Coach Lily exclaimed with a glance at the treat. She waved good-bye with a final "Take it easy, girls!"

The six spoons barely hit the table before the girls attacked.

Makena enjoyed the ice cream but noticed Chloe was hardly eating.

"Chloe, I'm so bummed you can't play this summer. Not even the second tournament?" she asked her friend.

Chloe shook her head. "I begged my parents, but they said no. I have too many performances."

"That's terrible," Makena said. The summer tournaments wouldn't be the same without Chloe, and Makena felt like she should say more, but she was distracted by a gob of flying hot fudge that landed with a thud on the table in front of her.

"Hey!" Makena cried. "The heck?"

She reached in with her spoon for a mouthful but was

swatted away. She looked to her right and came face-to-face with Jessie wielding her spoon like a samurai.

Makena smirked and took up her weapon.

• • •

Even though they often couldn't be at her games or tournaments, her parents did their best to support her obsession with soccer. She really wished her family was with her now in Philadelphia, but Makena's dad Rory was chef and owner of a gourmet shop, and it was really hard for him to get away on weekends. Makena's mother Stacey was an expert on butterflies and other insects, and Makena thought that made her mom both weird and kind of cool. But she was also super busy with her work. They kept promising they would eventually make it to one of the tournaments, but Makena had sort of gotten used to just being with her team.

Straightening out her blue-and-yellow Brookville Breakers uniform, Makena sized up the Westside team, who was stretching in a circle on the other side of the field. They looked as good as ever, she thought.

"Ready?" she asked Val, who was plopped on the ground beside her.

"You know I'm not," Val said.

Makena sighed and watched with amusement as her BFF went through her sacred pregame checklist. Makena knew it by heart. First, Val double-knotted her laces. Then she meticulously tucked the tips into the sides of her shoes. (Val couldn't stand it when her laces flopped around during a game.) Next, she fiddled with her shin guards, refolded her tube socks, and adjusted her headband. Several times.

"Ready now?" Makena asked, after the third headband adjustment.

"One last thing," Val answered, checking her cleats for dirt. "OK, ready."

"Finally!" Makena said, laughing and pulling Val to her feet, then dribbling quickly onto the field, making sharp moves to the left and right. Val was beside her in a second. Makena laid off a pass to the right without even looking. Val collected the ball and delivered it right back to Makena's foot. Neither girl ever broke stride. Always in rhythm. That's how it was between Mac and Val.

The two girls could not have looked more different though. Makena was tall, and Val was tiny. Makena was fair with Irish freckles and bright eyes that were a mix of green, blue, and yellow. Val was Mexican-American. Her skin was like cocoa, her hair was so black that in some lights it looked blue, and her big, brown eyes were steady and warm.

The two girls moved in tandem toward the rest of the Breakers, who were taking shots on goal.

"So what do you know about this new player?" Val asked Makena as they waited to take their turns.

"Not much," Makena said, pushing the ball to her right and firing a shot toward the goal.

"All I know is she's a midfielder. She's from New Jersey. And she's late," Makena said. She scanned the field for an unfamiliar face but just saw her regular squad warming up. Ariana was in goal, Jessie was trying to do some juggling, and the rest of the girls were starting a game of keep-away. Makena felt a pang of sadness for Chloe. She knew she wanted to be on the field with her friends.

"What kind of player comes late to a tournament?" Val asked with an annoyed tone. "The game's about to start."

"That's a good question," Makena said, looking around. "I guess we'll find out."

"Breakers! Bring it in!"

Coach Lily held up her clipboard with the lineup. Lily ran them through their positions and told them the new player, a girl named Skylar, was running late. Makena was still annoyed, but once the referee blew his whistle, she was swept away by the magic of the game.

The only problem was today's magic was more like a curse. It was one of those days when nothing was going their way. The ball wouldn't go in no matter how many shots they took. It was like there was an invisible screen in front of the goal. The ball hit the side posts and bounced into the goalie's hands. It sailed over the crossbar from impossible angles.

Bounce, bounce, bounce. Everywhere but into the back of the net.

Makena and the rest of her team were frustrated, and the game remained scoreless.

"Hey! I'm open!" a girl screamed. "Makena, give me the ball!"

It took a second for Makena to register that the person was calling to her. All her teammates just called her Mac. She passed the ball quickly, but her two-second delay was too much. Her pass was intercepted by a blur in black, and the ball went out of bounds.

"My bad," Makena called, apologizing for the pass. She ran over to take the throw. The girl jogged over to talk to her.

"Hey, you're Makena, right? I'm Skylar. I heard you're

really awesome. I'm playing right next to you. So, listen, I'm going to fake a run down the line but then go into the middle. You get me the ball, OK?"

Makena nodded, a little stunned. So this was her new teammate. She stared at Skylar's face.

"OK?" Skylar asked again.

"Got it." Makena nodded, waking up and hoping Skylar was just what the team needed to turn this game around.

Skylar had medium-length, spiky, dark hair that flapped like a bird's wing when she ran. She wore a tattered black headband to keep the hair out of her eyes, which Makena thought made her look ultra-fierce. On one side of her head, her hair was cut super short and had a stripe dyed scarlet. To top it off, she had a temporary tattoo on her lower arm that said *Glory*, and she wore black stuff under her eyes like a football player.

Skylar ran straight at Makena, and Makena faked the throw, and when the defender moved forward, she launched the ball over Skylar's head and into play.

Makena was psyched Skylar was on their side. She certainly wouldn't want to have to play against her.

Val made a run down the line. Makena smiled.

"Skylar!" Val called, darting quickly across the grass.

Skylar sent a beautiful lofting pass over the defense.

Val handled the high ball easily, bringing it down to her foot without losing speed. She took off toward the corner flags. Makena knew she was going to go for a cross.

A Westside defender ran out to meet Val. Val waited for the girl to get close, then pulled back her left foot like she was going for the cross. The fake worked. Val deftly dribbled around her to launch a cross. It was perfect, floating high above the defenders with enough backspin that Makena knew it would come down in front of the goal.

Makena moved forward, timing her jump.

Keeping her eyes glued on the ball, Makena launched herself into the air. A defender jumped with her, but Makena moved higher. The ball arrived; Makena flicked her head to the side. She felt it connect with the side of her head and heard the satisfying thump that sent it soaring toward the upper corner of the goal.

As she fell to the ground, she waited for the cheers to come. There was no way it hadn't gone in. She hit the grass with a thud but heard only a whistle and the referee's call.

"Corner kick!"

Corner kick? How could that be?

"What happened?" Makena stammered.

"Goalie tipped it out of bounds." Skylar was shaking her head. "Unbelievable."

Makena sprinted over to take the kick. She raised her hand to signal her teammates that she was ready. Skylar, Val, and Jessie all put their hands up in reply.

Lily had moved the whole team into offense. Makena drove the ball as hard as she could toward the goal. This wasn't a long, loopy pass but a hard-driven knuckler. She was hoping for any kind of deflection. There were so many girls crowded in front of the goal it was hard to see what was happening. First, the ball careened into the mix and bounced off the thigh of a defender. Jessie ran forward and tried to tap it in. The ball ricocheted off another Westside Wildcat. It was like soccer pinball.

Finally, Skylar came pushing through the crowd and, with her knee, corralled the ball into the goal. Makena heard the whistle blow and breathed a sigh of relief.

The Breakers were finally ahead.

Before the restart, the girls gathered in a huddle of sweaty excitement. Makena was nervous. Soccer is fickle. Things can change very quickly, particularly when one side thinks they have already won. The Westside parents were pacing and quiet. Their coach, a tall lady with curly red hair, had a determined look on her face.

A Westside striker, a firecracker of a player, kicked off, and Val gave chase. Makena watched as Val forced the forward to pass the ball behind her, keeping the pressure on. Jessie moved to support Val.

"I'm open," the Wildcat forward called.

The ball went rolling through the center of the field.

Makena pounced, collecting the pass easily and letting her momentum carry her forward. She touched the ball past one player and kept moving, always looking to make a pass or draw another defender to her. No one stepped up to challenge Makena for the ball, so she kept moving. She thought about a pass but knew the first rule of a good attacker: If you're open in front of the goal...*shoot*!

Makena wasn't going to miss this time. She moved to her left, ready to shoot—and felt her feet go out from under her. In a split second she went from about to score to a tangle on the ground, fighting to breathe. Someone had hit her from behind. The referee blew his whistle. He pointed to a spot on the ground just outside the box. Makena had been fouled. The Breakers would get a free kick.

Makena barely registered what was happening. She felt as if someone had stuck a vacuum cleaner tube in her mouth and sucked all the air out of her lungs. She couldn't get a breath. Val rushed over.

"You OK? I think you got the wind knocked out of

you," she said. "Put your arms over your head and take a deep breath."

Makena nodded and did what she was told. Slowly, her lungs started to refill. She felt awful. Her side ached. Skylar came over and whispered to Makena, "Nice work. Way to get the foul. Stay down for a minute more. Groan or something."

Makena still wasn't able to speak and could only give Skylar a puzzled look in reply.

"Do you need a break?" the referee asked Makena.

She shook her head. Val helped her to her feet and waved off their coach.

"I'm fine," she managed to croak. But she wasn't. "You better take the kick, Val."

Val grabbed the ball, lined up for the free kick, and waited for the referee's whistle. Makena had lost track of time. Would this game ever end?

Makena heard the beep and watched as Val's shot curled over Westside's wall, past the keeper but over the goal and out of bounds. She had missed. Makena remained doubled over in pain.

Coach Lily called for a substitution.

"Mac!" she called. Makena shook her head. She was feeling better, she told herself.

"Let's go, Coach," the referee said. "In or out."

The Westside goalie was ready to play. Their coach began to complain that Makena was wasting time. She tried to straighten up.

"Out," Coach Lily said. "Now."

Makena begrudgingly went to the sideline, and Jasmine came on in her place.

"Great playing, Mac," Coach Lily said. "Get some water. Take it easy. You took quite a hit."

Makena collapsed on the ground. Makena started to feel sick as she watched Westside come back. They moved down the field working as a team to string several beautiful passes together. A tall, thin winger, playing on the outside, took the ball all the way down to the corner flag. Makena struggled to get to her feet. She wanted to yell, "Stop her!" The words wouldn't come. A feeling of dread joined the cramp in her side.

Jessie, the Breakers' clutch defender, read Makena's mind and came in at the last minute. She blocked the cross. Somehow the ball deflected off the winger and went out of bounds.

Breakers' ball. Jasmine, the left midfielder, picked it up for the throw-in.

But Makena watched as Skylar sauntered over and

took the ball from Jasmine's hands. *What's she doing?* Makena wondered.

Skylar bent down to tie her shoe, black hair flopping over her headband. By now, the Westside coach's face was as red as her hair. Makena worried she was going to explode like some kind of cherry bomb.

"You've got to be kidding me!" the coach bellowed, pointing at Skylar.

"Play on!" the referee warned. Skylar kept tying her shoe.

"Jessie, go take it," Coach Lily yelled from the sidelines, with a shake of her head.

"Skylar, let's go." Jessie sprinted over, grabbed the ball from next to Skylar, and threw the ball up the line. Makena saw Skylar laugh and jog back onto the field.

"One minute left," Makena heard Lily try to encourage the girls. "Look alive, defense!"

Makena and the rest of the field suddenly heard a howl.

"Owww! My ankle!" It was Skylar. "I stepped in a hole!"

Makena watched, worried, as Skylar ripped off her black headband and rolled on the ground.

"Coach!" the referee called Coach Lily onto the field. After a few seconds, their coach helped Skylar limp to the sideline. She plopped down a few feet from Makena and gave her a wink.

"Abby," Lily called. She needed a substitute on the field. "Get ready. Quickly."

The referee had his hand on his watch. He was holding the time. Abby had already taken off her cleats. She thought the game was over.

"This is outrageous!" Makena heard one of the parents yell. She struggled to her feet. She could go in for the last minute of the game and just stand there.

Abby scrambled to get ready, but Skylar suddenly rolled over, ran to the sideline, and said, "Coach, I'm OK now!"

"What?" Coach Lily had a tense look on her face. "It's OK, Skylar. Just take a rest and get some ice."

"No, really. Look, I'm fine," Skylar said, jumping up and down to prove her point.

Coach Lily looked at Abby, who was still trying to jam her foot into her cleat. She sighed, "OK. Go. Now!"

The spectators booed as Skylar retook the field. She was running fine. Nothing was wrong with her ankle now. The referee took out a yellow card.

"What's that for, Coach?" Makena asked.

"For wasting time," Coach Lily answered in a low voice. Makena could hear disapproving murmurs from parents on the other side of the field.

The Wildcats gave one final push, but then time finally did run out. Makena collapsed in a heap when she heard the whistle blow.

3

"V ictory!" Makena shouted across the messy hotel room. "Can I have this tattoo?"

"Sure." Skylar nodded. "Victory. That's what it's all about, right?"

Makena ripped the word from a colorful sheet of temporary tattoos. Vaulting a pile of dirty soccer clothes, she ran into the small bathroom to get some water while Val and Jessie sorted through the rest of the tattoo choices.

"How long do I have to hold it?" Makena yelled.

"Fifteen minutes," Skylar answered.

"Fifteen minutes?" Makena came out of the bathroom with a wet washcloth on her arm.

"I'm kidding." Skylar laughed. "Sucker!"

Makena scowled.

"Just, like, thirty seconds," Skylar said, still chuckling.

"Love the look on your face. Just be sure to lift the paper off slowly so it doesn't tear."

"Look at this one," Jessie said, holding up a flaming soccer ball. "This one is like your shot today, Val."

Val smiled and asked. "How long do they stay on again?"

"A couple of days, depending on how many showers you take and how sweaty you get."

"What do you think?" Makena asked, showing off her right arm. Bright-green and orange letters covered her skin.

"Oh, love it," Skylar said. "We're going to kill 'em tomorrow."

"Can you believe the looks that team was giving us at the buffet?" Makena asked.

"I didn't know all the teams were staying in the same hotel," Jessie said. Coming face-to-face with the Baton Ridge Thunder at dinner that night had caught most of the girls by surprise. The Breakers had won their second game of the Philadelphia Freedom Tournament easily, and now they would face the Thunder in the morning. The winner would be on to the finals.

"The whole tournament is staying here," Skylar told them.

"The girl in the salad line looked like she wanted you for dinner," Jessie said.

"Oh, whatev," Skylar said.

"Do you know them?" Val asked.

"Nah, not really. I might have seen one or two of them at a soccer camp or something like that."

"They seemed to know *you*," Val said in a voice that Makena recognized. Val was not digging Skylar.

If Skylar noticed, it didn't slow her down. "My dad says their regional ranking is below ours."

"Regional ranking? What does that mean?" Val asked.

"Oh, you get points when you play in a tournament, and the better you do, the higher you are ranked. My dad tracks all this stuff on his computer."

Makena shrugged. She'd never heard of rankings for soccer teams, and the thought of either of her parents having any idea how to look up that information made her chuckle a little bit. She was about to say so when a loud knock on the door interrupted her. All four girls squeaked in surprise.

"Anyone hooomme?" Jasmine's mother, Mrs. Manikas, asked, sticking her head into the room.

"Hi," the girls answered in unison. Mrs. Manikas was the team mom and their chaperone for the night. Makena, Skylar, Jessie, and Val had been assigned the hotel room that connected to the one that Mrs. Manikas shared with

Jasmine, Ella, and Abby. The rest of the Breakers were with their parents in rooms down the hall.

"I'm collecting stinky socks. Anyooooone?" Mrs. Manikas said. Pinching her nose, she looked around the room with disgust. There were muddy shoes on the beds, clothes pouring out of duffel bags, soccer balls and shin guards strewn on the floor, and one particularly alarming puddle on the worn rug in front of the television.

Jasmine's mom bent down to investigate.

"Melted Popsicle," Makena offered. "Pink lemonade."

Mrs. Manikas nodded and took a few steps back.

"You girls need to clean that up. Also, please give me your dirty uniforms from today, and I'll throw them in the laundry. I'll wash them tonight and have them for you by six thirty tomorrow morning. OK? Breakfast is at seven o'clock in the lobby, so be sure to come dressed to go."

The girls scrambled to gather their belongings while Skylar made a halfhearted effort to soak up the Popsicle she had spilled on the rug. Pieces of grass floated to the carpet from Makena's socks as she handed them over.

"They're still a little wet," Makena said. "Just sweat. I think."

Mrs. Manikas backed out of the room holding a pile of uniforms.

"Lights out in half an hour. Big game tomorrooooow!" Mrs. Manikas sung.

"OK," the girls replied.

Skylar closed the door behind her. "Oh, so glad she's goooone," she said, and all four Breakers collapsed in giggles.

"Man, I'm so sore," Jessie said, rubbing her thighs.

"Me too," Makena agreed. Her legs hurt when she walked, sat, lay down. She plopped down on the bed next to Val and admired her new tattoo.

"This is nothing, girls," Skylar said. "When you go to ODP, you have, like, three practices a day, and then you hit the gym. Now's *that's* how you get sore."

"What's ODP?" Jessie asked.

"What's ODP? Are you kidding me? ODP is the Olympic Development Program. You know, where they pick the girls for the national team? Carli Lloyd? Alex Morgan? Hello?"

Jessie shrugged her shoulders, clearly embarrassed.

"You need to start learning about the real world of soccer if you want to be taken seriously," Skylar went on. She had Makena's full attention. Makena wanted to play soccer for the rest of her life. She wanted to score in the World Cup. She wanted to win a gold medal at the Olympics. She wanted to make it to the top, and if Skylar could help her get there, she was all ears.

"There are definitely going to be some big-time scouts at this game tomorrow."

"Scouts for what?" Makena asked.

"College," Skylar said solemnly.

"College! We're not even in eighth grade," Makena said.

"Yeah, college. If you aren't on the recruiting radar by eighth grade, you might as well just forget it. That's what my dad says."

"Come on, Skylar." Val rolled her eyes. "That's ridiculous."

"Is it?" Skylar replied. "Mark my words, they'll be there tomorrow, and they'll be watching. Which is why we have to win. No matter what."

"No matter what?" Val muttered, shaking her head. She jumped off the bed, grabbed her toothbrush, and headed for the bathroom. As she pushed open the door, she leaned back and asked, "Hey, Skylar, how's your ankle?"

Val closed the bathroom door behind her without waiting for an answer. Skylar ignored the question and motioned for Makena and Jessie to come closer.

"I saw an awesome hot tub out behind the restaurant," she whispered.

"Yeah, so?" Makena asked.

"Let's go check it out. We can loosen up our sore muscles. It'll be perfect."

"It's pitch-black out there," Jessie said.

"Exactly. We'll have it all to ourselves."

"Mrs. M is never going to let us go," Makena pointed out.

"Who said we're going to ask? We just have to wait until everyone's asleep."

"We'll get in so much trouble," Jessie whispered.

"It's only a crime if you get caught," Skylar said. "And we're not going to get caught. Trust me, all the big players warm down in a hot tub. It's just what we need."

Makena Walsh's heart thwacked in her chest like the churning blades of a helicopter. She and Val were sharing a bed, and somehow, her friend was sleeping soundly. Makena couldn't imagine how all the jumping and thudding her heart was doing wasn't keeping her friend awake. She was grateful Val was sleeping though, because she knew she would be really upset with her for even considering sneaking out of their hotel room, much less going without her.

Was Skylar brave enough to really do it?

Sure, Makena wanted to soothe her sore muscles like a pro, but she'd never done anything like sneak out before. She'd never even contemplated doing anything like that. Makena saved her most daring exploits and moments for the field.

This was so unlike her.

But it was also exciting. Skylar was exciting. Makena loved her cool tattoos. She envied Skylar's wild hair. Skylar was different, in the best kind of way. Makena gathered a section of her own strawberry-blond hair around her finger as she lay in the bed. For games, she always wore a long ponytail or, when she was feeling crazy, two French braids. Next to Skylar, Makena's hair was basic and boring. How was a college coach going to notice Makena next to someone like Skylar?

Val rolled over. Makena could tell Val didn't like Skylar. Val wasn't very good at hiding her feelings. Was what Skylar had done during the first game really that wrong? So she tied her shoe at the end. Big whoop. It's dangerous to play with your shoelaces undone. And she twisted her ankle. Not her fault she stepped in a hole. Makena thought Val was being a little hard on Skylar.

Makena adjusted her pillow and felt a twinge in her side. She hurt all over. Getting the wind knocked out of her was an awful experience. Maybe it would be good to relax in a nice, warm tub. Makena felt herself calming down, the helicopter circling in to land. Yawning, she pulled the covers over her shoulder and nestled down into the soft sheets. The room was pitch-black and quiet.

She was pretty sure Jessie and Skylar were already

asleep and wouldn't be going after all. *Well, it would have been fun*, Makena thought. *I'm brave too.* She closed her eyes and started to doze off, relieved she didn't have to prove it.

She didn't feel the first poke. The second one made her sit straight up.

"What?" Makena cried out.

"Sh," Skylar said. "Here."

Makena's eyes adjusted to the darkness, and she saw Skylar and Jessie standing over her bed. Val shifted slightly next to her. Makena noticed Skylar and Jessie both had streaks of black under their eyes.

"Is that eye black?" she asked.

"Let's move," Jessie ordered.

"Here," Skylar said again, shoving something into Makena's hands.

"What's this?"

"T-shirt and shorts. Unless you want to go naked? I don't have a bathing suit. Do you?"

"Oh, right," Makena said. Silently, she changed her clothes. "What time is it?"

"Midnight."

Makena realized she must have fallen asleep.

Jessie poked her head out into the hallway. "Coast

is clear," she said softly. Makena suddenly imagined her teammate with a career in the military.

The three girls crept silently down the hall to the stairs. Their room was on the fourth floor. Quickly, the trio found themselves in the lobby. The receptionist was busy on her phone and didn't seem to notice the three barefoot girls scurrying by. They found the door that said *Patio* and slipped outside. It was that easy.

Hot vapor swirled invitingly in the cool night. Skylar went first, making a face that said the water was scalding hot as she slid slowly into the Jacuzzi.

"Ahh," she whispered. "Now that's awesome."

Makena and Jessie climbed the steps. Makena paused before getting in. She looked around but saw only potted plants. She heard muted voices from people in the parking lot behind the hotel.

"Get in," Skylar urged.

Jessie went next. Then Makena slipped her foot into the steaming water.

"Ow!" Makena cried, yanking her foot back. She hadn't been in too many hot tubs in her life. "That's hot! Really hot."

"You get used to it," Skylar said, lounging in the corner, her arms resting on the sides.

Makena tried again. She could not believe people did this on purpose. Her skin was going to fall off. Jessie, the budding Navy SEAL, didn't seem to be having any problem, Makena noticed.

"Since you're up," Skylar said, "how about turning on the jets? The button is right behind you."

Makena reached back, hit the green button, and saw the pool come to life. Skylar and Jessie immediately started trapping bubbles in their T-shirts and shorts. *It's now or never*, Makena thought. She marched down the first few steps, sucked in her breath, and slowly sank down in the water.

"This. Is. The. Life," Skylar sighed, her head tilted back, hair sticking up in front like a tuft of grass.

Makena had to agree. "I feel like a celebrity," she said, moving closer to one of the jets. "Plus, I really do think this is helping my muscles."

"I wonder what the Thunder will be like tomorrow. I hear they're really tough," Jessie said.

"Me too," Makena agreed.

"It'll be a piece of cake," Skylar said. "They have matching bags and stuff. They think that makes them good or something."

Makena turned to the side to massage her sore back. "Man, that really hurt today."

"Yeah, but you got us the free kick. That's all that matters," Skylar said.

"How *is* your ankle?" Makena asked. "Did you step in a hole or something?"

Skylar rubbed her leg and smiled. "I saw that in a USA–Brazil game. It must have eaten up at least the last three minutes."

"You mean you didn't really step in a hole?" Jessie asked.

"Look, all the pros do it. Don't you guys watch soccer on TV? When you're ahead, you've got to do what it takes to eat up the last few minutes of a game. It's called gamesmanship. I didn't make it up."

Of course Makena watched the World Cups, men's and women's. There *was* a lot of falling down in the final minutes, no question about it. It just had never occurred to her that it was something U13 girls could do.

"But, Skylar, isn't that cheating?" Makena blurted out.

"Getting hurt isn't cheating, Makena. It's a totally expected part of soccer. Just remember, when you get hurt, even a little, roll on the ground and act like your leg is about to fall off. That way you'll get the free kick or the penalty kick. Everyone does it. If you want to play soccer like the pros, you better do what the pros do. That's how you win."

Makena and Jessie shared a look. Coach Lily had

never told them to do anything like that. Makena shifted to massage the other side of her back as she thought. Skylar seemed so sure of herself. And she seemed to know what she was talking about with the ODP stuff, rankings, and college coaches.

Makena didn't know what to think. She traced the outline of the tattoo on her arm. *Victory.*

Makena was opening her mouth to tell Skylar she didn't really think the Breakers were into faking injuries when she heard loud footsteps approaching. She looked past the bushes and saw the beam of a strong flashlight bobbing on the path to the hot tub.

"Someone's coming!" Makena said.

"Kill the jets," Skylar whispered to Jessie. Jessie jumped out of the Jacuzzi and hit the red button. The hot tub went silent, which only made the footsteps seem louder.

"Hey!" they heard a deep voice yell. "Hot tub closed at ten."

It was hotel security. A tall man with a serious scowl was approaching. Jessie stood dripping on the patio, eye black smudged across her face.

This was not good.

"What are you doing over there?" he yelled. "This is private property. Don't move."

Jessie's newfound confidence seemed to fly out the window. She looked at Makena. Then at Skylar. Makena and Skylar's eyes met, and they yelled to Jessie as loudly as they could.

"*Ruuuuun!*"

J essie took off like a rocket. Makena saw her make a
drippy beeline for the rear lobby door. You couldn't
miss the squish of her wet clothes and the slap of her feet
as she scurried down the path. Makena followed Skylar's
lead and slunk back into the water as the security guard
trudged past.

"Hang on there!" He puffed after Jessie, not focusing
on the other two girls in the hot tub.

"Let's go the other way," Skylar said.

Makena and Skylar slipped out of the hot tub and ran
up the path toward the parking lot, the way the guard had
approached. They both peered over their shoulders to see if
he was following them.

"Oh man," Makena said, "I hope Jessie made it inside."

"No kidding," Skylar said. "She'd turn us in in a second."

Makena slowed to a quick walk. The parking lot was on their left, and the hotel was on the right. Everything seemed calm. Now all she could hear was the tiny pitter-patter of water drops trailing from their shorts and hair.

"How are we going to get back in?" Makena asked.

"I say we go around the front and wait for everything to calm down. We can sneak back into the lobby and up the stairs," Skylar answered.

The girls moved past a group of fragrant hedges encircling a light post. As they emerged from the shadows, Skylar's eyes widened.

"Oh, lookey what we have here."

It was a golf cart but an awesome version. There were doors on the sides, windshield wipers, headlights, and even an iPod holder. *Security* was stenciled in bright-orange letters across the front.

"Ever drive one of these?" Skylar asked.

"I've never even seen one like this," Makena said, running her hand along the fiberglass fender.

"Get in," Skylar said.

"Are you nuts?" Makena asked, backing away.

Skylar smiled and didn't answer. She climbed into the driver's seat and began fiddling with the buttons on the snazzy dash.

Makena leaned in, looked around, and said, "Skylar, you're getting everything all wet. Let's go."

Suddenly, the radio came to life, startling Makena. "Canvassing rear parking lot. Over."

Makena looked at the back of the hotel. And all the cars.

"Uh, Skylar…" she said.

"Check out these seats!" Skylar said.

"Skylar, I think this is the rear…"

"I think this is leather!"

"…parking lot!" Makena was frantic. She heard footsteps again. "Skylar, let's go!"

Skylar didn't budge.

The footsteps got louder.

"Skylar, someone's coming!"

Makena looked over the roof of the golf cart and saw the guard running toward them from the front of the hotel. Makena turned to run, but Skylar kept fiddling around by the steering wheel.

"Step away from the vehicle!" a voice yelled. Makena grabbed Skylar by the arm and tried to pull her out of the golf cart. This was getting out of hand. Makena just wanted to get out of there, find Jessie, and get back in bed where they belonged.

"*Get in!*" Skylar yelled. Makena's mouth hung open as

she saw Skylar pull the gearshift. *Beep. Beep. Beep.* The golf cart began to move in reverse.

"*Skylar, no!*" Makena chased the cart as it pulled away.

"He'll catch us on foot, Makena!" Skylar shouted. "Come on!"

Makena shook her head in disbelief, turned, and sprinted back up the path. She dove behind a row of hedges, too scared to do anything but watch.

"Get back here!" the guard yelled. His face was contorted with anger and exertion. Skylar took off like Danica Patrick on an Indy 500 straightaway. The out-of-shape guard bent over to catch his breath and then jogged after her into the parking lot.

He would never have caught them on foot.

A few seconds later, she heard the cart approach. Skylar was circling back. A second guard had joined the chase. *Uh-oh, this guy is much faster*, Makena thought. Skylar sped closer, zooming past the cars in the lot. The guard tried to block her. Makena saw Skylar grin and hook a sharp left toward the Jacuzzi. She careened smoothly away from him and headed straight for the hotel.

But Makena could tell she was going too fast. Skylar shrieked as the golf cart clipped the curb and started to spin. Makena held her breath as Skylar launched herself from the driver's seat a second before the cart crashed into a sprinkler head. A wet rainbow of water exploded into the night sky.

Skylar took off toward the hotel, and Makena followed her, desperate to get back to her room. She could hear the guards yelling loudly, but a quick look over her shoulder told her they were too busy dealing with the broken water pipe and crashed golf cart to care about them.

Makena and Skylar snuck back inside the lobby and went quietly up the stairs. On the fourth floor, they found a frightened Jessie hiding in the stairwell.

"Makena! Skylar! Oh my God!" Jessie shrieked. "What happened out there?"

Makena started to explain about the wild golf cart chase, but before she could get the words out, Skylar started to laugh.

"Did…did…did…you see the look on that guy's face when he was chasing me?" Skylar gasped between breaths. "Man, I thought he was going to split his pants."

She grabbed her sides, tears streaming down her face. Her laughter was contagious. Jessie started to giggle. Despite herself, Makena started to laugh along with them, her fear releasing itself in a fit of nervous giggles.

"I can't believe you took his golf cart!" Makena yelled. "That was unreal!"

"You did *what*?" Jessie asked.

"Skylar took the security guards' cart, and they chased her all over the parking lot!"

Jessie stopped laughing, slack-jawed. "Are you kidding me? Skylar, are you crazy?"

"Relax," Skylar said.

"Relax?" Jessie said. "When they find us, we're dead meat! We'll be kicked off the team, arrested, suspended, grounded…you name it!"

"They're not going to find us."

Makena felt her thudding helicopter heart taking off again. What if Jessie was right?

"They're not going to find us," Skylar repeated, "because they aren't going to tell anyone what happened."

"What do you mean?" Makena asked.

"Well, for starters, do you think those two guards are going to admit that some girl stole their golf cart and made them look like idiots?"

Makena wasn't convinced. "But what if they do? You crashed the cart into a sprinkler!"

"She what!?" Jessie lay down across three stairs and covered her eyes with her hands. "Oh no, oh no, oh no."

Makena nodded.

Skylar didn't blink. "There are, like, two hundred

soccer-playing girls staying here. They could never prove it was us."

Jessie looked at Makena. Makena looked at Jessie. Jessie started to giggle again. "She stole a golf cart?"

Makena smiled. "It was pretty crazy. But kind of cool."

Skylar stood up and offered Makena a hand. "*Kind of* cool? It was awesome. Come on, Makena, live a little. And remember," Skylar said, flashing Makena a big smile, "it's only a crime if you get caught."

6

"Hustle over, Mac!" Coach Lily called from in front of the goal. Makena fumbled with her shoelaces and tried to catch up with the rest of her team. The Breakers were already divided into two groups and starting a warm-up game of keep-away.

"I'm here, Coach," Makena said as she joined the closer group. She, Jessie, and Skylar shared a conspiratorial smile. So far, it seemed Skylar was right. No SWAT team had descended on the hotel in search of hot tub–loving soccer players. There was no APB out on a stolen golf cart. Nothing. The sprinkler was off. The hotel was quiet.

"Not there, Mac," Lily said. "You're in this group."

"Oh," said Makena, covering up a yawn. She moved to the second group of players. Val was in the middle of a circle trying to win the ball from the girls on the outside. *It's a good thing Val's such a sound sleeper*, Makena thought, watching her friend zoom tirelessly after the ball. The three Breakers had snuck back into the room, trying to stifle their giggles, dry off, and slip back into bed without waking Val or Jasmine's mother in the next room over.

Makena reacted a little too late to Jasmine's pass. As she moved for the ball, Val popped in between them and stole it.

"You're in the middle, Mac," Val said, giving Makena a weird look. A pang of guilt struck Makena in the gut for keeping secrets from her best friend.

Makena moved to the inside of the circle, like she'd done countless times before. Usually she could intercept a pass on the second or third try. Today the girls' passes were really sharp.

Or she was really slow.

"Time-out," Makena called. Her shoelace was undone again. Makena bent down and for the first time noticed how crowded the field was. Parents, coaches, and several of the other teams in the tournament were getting comfortable on the sidelines.

There was a large red-and-black sign that read, *THE THUNDER IS READY TO RUMBLE.* There was even a hot dog stand and ice cream truck set up by the road.

Makena was noticing that this tournament *was* a big deal. The competitions near Brookville, a town just north of New York City, felt much smaller. *Skylar was right—this really is the big time*, she thought to herself.

"Do you need some kind of special invitation today, Mac?" a voice asked.

She looked up to see Coach towering above her.

"My shoelaces were untied," she explained.

"Again?"

"Again," Makena answered, trying to tie faster, which only caused the laces to jumble into an impressive knot.

Coach Lily sighed and knelt down next to her.

"Girls, keep passing," she said to the Breakers. To Makena, she asked, "What's with you today, Mac? You nervous or something?"

"No, not at all," Makena answered. And she wasn't. She had been so busy reliving what was by far the most thrilling night of her life that the game had barely crossed her mind.

"Listen, the Thunder is known for its passing. They're really excellent at controlling the ball and moving it around. So you're going to have to work hard and be patient to win the ball and feed it up to the offense."

"OK. Got it," Makena said, bopping back into the

warm-up. She won after a few tries, but she was huffing and puffing by the time the referee blew his whistle to indicate the game was about to start. Makena searched for Jessie and Skylar but saw they were taking a water break on the sidelines. Makena took her place on the field and willed herself to focus.

From kickoff, she could tell that Lily wasn't kidding about the Thunder. They had her going in circles. The two tall midfielders, in particular, were incredible. One seemed to have Velcro on her cleats, and the other just never missed. They passed the ball better than any team she'd ever faced, and Makena had to work constantly to even get a foot on it. Her legs were starting to feel like they were filled with sand. Skylar took a few weak shots, but they went wide. Val hadn't even gotten the ball.

For Makena, soccer was normally the sharpest part of her life. Every minute of a match played out in her mind as clearly as crystal. The sights, smells, and noises of a game formed a rainbow of soccer joy and excitement in her memory. But today she was in a fog. Makena couldn't get moving. She couldn't anticipate where the ball was going. Time was flying, and she kept waiting for something to change.

But all that changed was the score.

The Thunder went up 1 to 0 off a corner kick in the first minute of the second half.

"Come on," Val encouraged the team before the restart. "We've got this."

Skylar, Jessie, and Makena nodded like zombies.

Makena pushed herself harder. She surged forward and intercepted a pass in midfield. Val was moving down the line, and Makena sent a long pass to the corner. Skylar and Makena made runs for the goal. But this time they didn't communicate, and they both ended up on the near post. Val's cross went long, and there was no Breaker in place to track it.

The ball flew across the face of the goal untouched as Makena and Skylar backpedaled to chase it down. The Thunder defender moved to clear the ball but miscalculated and hit it wrong. The ball soared straight up into the air.

The tall Thunder sweeper called out, "I got it!" and moved to clear the ball with a header. But her teammates didn't move out of the way. She collided with another girl, leaving the ball bouncing awkwardly in the box.

Val, the closest Breaker, tried to take the shot, but her half volley went spinning backward right toward the face of the midfielder with Velcro cleats. The girl raised her hand reflexively just before the ball smacked her right in the nose.

The field froze. The whistle blew.

Hand ball in the box. Automatic penalty kick.

This was the Breakers' big chance. Maybe their only chance.

"Mac!" Makena heard Lily call from the sideline, but she was already searching for the ball. Makena always took the penalty kicks.

"You want me to take it?" Skylar offered.

"Nah, I got this," Makena said, realizing that Skylar didn't know Mac was the kicker.

The referee cleared the stunned Thunder players from the box, and the goalie took her place in the middle of goal. The ref gathered the ball, handed it to Makena, and said, "Wait for my whistle."

Makena nodded. She rolled the ball in her hands, dusting off a tiny tuft of grass. She knew that the goalie was watching her. She knew that she was checking her gloves and getting ready to guess which way Makena was going to shoot. Makena knew better than to look at her. Even more importantly, she knew to never, ever look at the side you were aiming for.

Instead, Makena envisioned the shot in her head like she had done so many times before. She would go to the lower-right corner.

She placed the ball on the penalty spot twelve yards out, careful to keep her eyes down, and focused on the ball.

Makena could see just the goalie's feet. She noticed that the girl seemed to be standing a little bit to the right of the middle of the goal.

Was the goalie crowding Makena's shot? Did she know Makena always went right?

Don't look, Makena told herself. *Just hit it, like you always do.*

But at the last second Makena couldn't help herself. She broke her own rule. Her brain was muddled, and she stole a glance at the goalie.

Their eyes met.

Makena's eyes darted to the right.

Immediately, she cast her eyes back down to the ground. *She saw me looking to that right corner*, Makena thought. *Do I have to go left now? No, no. I'll go right.*

The referee drew the whistle to his mouth, and a sharp quick beep filled the expectant air.

Makena stepped forward to take the kick, a few paces to the left of the ball. She'd hit it with her instep, straight into the lower-right corner, just like she always did.

She kept her eyes down, but in her peripheral vision,

she could see the goalie bouncing up and down on her line. *She knows I'm going right*, Makena thought.

"Play!" she heard the referee yell.

Makena stepped up to take the shot, moving deliberately to keep the ball low and hard. But at the last second she changed her mind and decided to go to the left corner. The problem was she was too far to the left of the ball. Her timing was wrong.

Everything was wrong.

Makena moved forward and hit the ball straight down the middle. It landed with a thud in the goalie's stomach. She'd saved it.

Makena had missed the penalty kick.

The relieved goalie punted the ball high, and Makena moved slowly back up the field, her mental haze returning.

The rest of the game zipped by. Before she knew it, the final whistle blew.

The Thunder erupted in celebration as the Breakers walked tiredly back to the bench.

Lily was there to welcome them each with a pat on the back.

"You girls gave it your all out there. I'm very proud of you. You worked hard. Now, hold your heads high and go out and congratulate them on a good win."

Makena trudged out to shake hands with the other team. She raised her eyes only to be faced with the jubilant smiles of the victorious Thunder. Their coaches and parents were beaming with pride from the sidelines, while the Breaker fans clapped with polite disappointment.

Makena replayed the missed penalty kick. In her mind, images of the kick mixed with images from the previous night. Guilt washed over her. She moved slowly to join her team, her head held low, eyes fixed on the ground.

Suddenly, she just wanted to go home. Soccer had never felt like this before.

Three reds, five blues, and one black," Makena told her mother, holding up a hodgepodge of mismatched soccer socks.

"All right, so let's get rid of one blue and one red and the lone black," her mom suggested.

"Get rid of them?" Makena asked, shocked, gathering up all the socks in her arms.

"If you toss the odd ones, you can make pairs of the others."

"But I need all of them." Makena gave her mother a look.

Her mother sighed and grimaced at the mess on the floor. "Mac, you've got to learn to let go of things. Look at these shorts. They must be five sizes too small! Put them in the donation pile."

"But, Mom, I scored my first goal in these!"

"Oh, Makena. If you want my help cleaning your room, you have to give up some of this junk."

Makena stared at her mother in shock. Junk? These were her prized possessions.

"Mom, this isn't even my room, remember?" As Makena spoke, she saw the look on her mother's face and instantly regretted her words.

"How can I forget when you remind me every hour on the hour?" Makena's mom responded in a sharp tone.

Makena quieted and went back to sorting socks, reluctantly placing the odd ones in the donation pile. She kept the shorts though. Why did she have to bring up the room situation? Last fall, she had to move into her brother's bedroom when their grandfather, Papa, came to live with them. Papa was old and needed a room with a bathroom, so Makena reluctantly gave up hers. At first, she was miserable about the change, but she'd come to enjoy her grandfather. Who knew an eighty-year-old could love *America's Got Talent* as much as she did? Even sharing a room with Will wasn't as bad as she'd thought it would be. Almost every night they read comic books together and told knock-knock jokes until laughter made their stomachs hurt and their parents started yelling from downstairs.

Makena watched as her mom pulled another pile of random items out from under the bunk beds. The past few months had added worry lines to her mom's face. Recently, Papa had developed a terrible cough that wouldn't go away. Her parents had had to take him to about a zillion doctors. Mom and Dad hadn't really told Makena and her brother Will much about what was going on, but they knew it wasn't great news.

"What about these?" Makena's mom held up a pair of princess pajama pants that must have been for a four-year-old. "You win any big tournaments with these on, Cinderella?"

Makena laughed, grabbed the pants, and threw them in the donation pile. "See, I can get rid of things!"

"Oh, very good," her mom said. Smiling, she got up from the floor. "My show starts in an hour. I have to get ready. We're dissecting a Palos Verdes Blue, which is…"

"The rarest butterfly in the world," Makena dutifully replied.

"Very good. Thought to be extinct for more than a decade, you know. That is going to be a big event on BugsAreCool.com."

Makena's mom kissed Makena on the top of her head and left the room. Her new web show, *Butterfly CSI*, was a hit in the bug universe.

"You going to watch?" her mom called back over her shoulder.

"Yeah, Mom," Makena said. "I'll watch it on the computer downstairs."

Makena went back to the chaos on the floor but quickly lost interest. She looked around for something else to do. *I'm so bored,* she thought. *Bored and lonely. I'm so bored and lonely I have to tell myself I'm bored and lonely.*

From the first day of school, Makena longed for summer to arrive. Now that it was here, she couldn't wait for it to be over. Val was in Texas visiting relatives, and Chloe was in an all-day ballet camp in New York City. Since the Memorial Day tournament, soccer was mostly done, and Makena found the days to be hot, empty, and endless.

Her next soccer event was the upcoming Fourth of July tournament, but that was still almost a week away. Makena flopped down on Will's bottom bunk and gazed up at her favorite poster of the U.S. women's national soccer team plastered above the desk. The USA players were in their white uniforms, arms wrapped around one another, sweaty and happy after another victory.

Makena hadn't touched a soccer ball since she'd returned from Philadelphia, and she'd never told Val about her Skylar adventures. She tried not to think about the loss or the missed penalty kick, but she stifled a laugh when she remembered the security guards trying to catch Skylar in the parking lot. *She really is brave,* Makena thought. *And she was right: We didn't get caught.*

Just then, Makena heard a ping from under a pile of sweatpants. It was her new cell phone.

Ping! Makena rummaged through the pile, knocking over shirts her mother had folded that morning, sending them flying into the air like popcorn. Val didn't have a cell phone yet, and Chloe wasn't allowed to text during her dance camp. Who could it be?

When Makena finally found the little black phone, she didn't recognize the number. The area code was 201.

Where is that? Makena wondered. But it didn't take her long to figure out who the sender was.

Been to any good hot tubs lately?

It had to be Skylar.

Makena was excited to get a text but couldn't imagine how Skylar had gotten her number. She asked her.

Coach was the immediate reply. Psyched 2 play in 7/4 tourney.

Well, that'll take care of my boredom, Makena thought. Suddenly, her phone rang. She nearly dropped it in surprise.

"Hello," she answered.

"It's me, Skylar. How's it going?"

"Good," Makena said. "But actually really boring."

"Yeah, me too," Skylar said. "Nothing going on here either."

"If you were here, we could go kick around," Makena said. There was a brief pause, and then Skylar spoke.

"Well, maybe I could come over and show you some of the cool moves I've been working on."

"Are you serious?" Makena asked. "That would be awesome!"

"Totally. There's a practice this week to get ready for the Canada trip, and I was thinking I could stay and hang out or something."

"Oh yeah, I didn't know you were coming to practice. Let me go ask my mom. But she loves all my Soccer Sisters, and I bet she'll say yes."

"So I'm a Soccer Sister now?"

"Of course! You're on the team, right?"

Makena didn't give Skylar time to answer. "Call you right back," she said. She ended the call and sprinted to find her mother before she started filming.

"Mom!" she yelled, galloping down the hallway. "Mom!"

"What! What is it?" her mom answered, instantly

worried. "Why are you yelling? Are you hurt?" Makena's mom always thought Makena was hurt.

"No, I'm fine. I need to ask you something."

"Not now, I'm about to go on the air." She was preparing her dissection tools.

"No, I need to ask you something supremely important."

"Can it wait?" her mom asked, turning back to her work.

"Mom. Pleeeeease. My friend Skylar from soccer wants to come and spend the night. Can she, Mom? Please, please, please?"

"*Mac*, I don't have time for this right now."

"Please just say yes, Mom. She can stay in Will's room with me. I'll donate clothes. Clean the whole house. Everything. Anything. I promise. I'll be nice to Will. I'll let Papa watch his shows. Please just say yes."

Makena's mom shook her head in resignation.

"I have a lot of work this week, and your grandfather isn't feeling very well. I have to take him back to the pulmonologist. I don't have time to entertain you and your new friend. Who is she anyway? I don't know that name."

"Mom, she's the *amazing* player I told you about. She's, like, on the national team or something. We won't be any trouble, Mom, I promise. We'll just go to practice and hang out. She's going to show me some cool moves. Please just say yes."

"OK," she said with a sigh.

"OK? That's a yes? She can come?"

"Yes, that's a yes. She can come. But please understand there's a lot going on and I need you girls to entertain yourselves."

"We will, I promise."

8

Makena had to cut quite a deal with her nine-year-old brother, Will, to convince him to sleep on the couch. She had to clear his dishes for a week, help him finish his endless Lego Death Star, and catch twenty-five fireflies. Plus she had her usual chores: She had to vacuum the living room, organize her books, pull weeds, and wash windows at Rosa's, her father's shop downtown. She was going to be busy, but she knew it was totally worth it to have Skylar come and visit.

Makena laughed when her dad saw Skylar's hair for the first time and did a double take. The magenta stripe was now bright green, and the tips of the short, cropped part were neon yellow. But Skylar won him over quickly by being a great eater and complimenting his cooking. Food was the fastest way to Rory Walsh's heart.

Skylar even played a few heated games of backgammon with Papa, who was surprisingly crafty. Things did get a little testy when Skylar and Papa didn't agree on who should get sent home on *Survivor*, but it had been a good visit so far. Makena was relieved Skylar didn't want to sneak out of the house or anything crazy like that.

"Mom, can we go to town today after practice?" Makena asked at breakfast.

"That's a great idea," her mom answered. "I have to take Papa to the doctor anyway."

"Can I come?" Will asked Makena and Skylar. "I want to get the new *Asterix* comic from Longo's Store."

Makena was about to answer yes when Skylar came out with a lie.

"Oh, Will, we'd love for you to come, but I think some of the Breakers are meeting up in town to work on our community service projects. It'll be so boring for you."

Makena's eyes went wide. There was no meeting and no community service planned that she knew about. Just practice at noon. But she nodded along with the story.

Makena's mom spoke up. "Yeah, Will, let them have some girl time. Girls, I love the idea of community service projects. Was that yours, Skylar?"

"Well, not entirely. The whole team wants to give back," Skylar lied.

"How wonderful," Makena's mom said. "So, Makena, please keep your phone close and check in with your father when you're in town. We'll be back this afternoon."

"OK, Mom," Makena answered guiltily.

•   •   •

The walk to Brookville was just a few blocks. Makena was excited to show Skylar around. Makena thought Brookville was a beautiful town, full of cute shops and cafés. It had an old-fashioned main street with a park, a soda fountain, Longo's comic store, and, of course, her dad's shop, Rosa's. Makena was saving that for after practice, when they could get anything they wanted there for free.

Practice was at the school field during the summers—just a ten-minute walk from Makena's house.

"This is a nice place," Skylar said.

"Yeah." Makena shrugged it off, but in truth she was proud of her little town.

"Have you ever played in the Roberts Cup?" Makena asked Skylar. The Roberts Cup was the tournament they were going to the coming weekend in Toronto.

"Oh sure, I played there last year. There are a lot of top coaches from colleges who come to watch," Skylar answered.

"Why aren't you playing with your old team anymore?" Makena wanted to know.

"You guys are better. They weren't going to the tournament this summer, and my dad says I need better exposure."

Makena was surprised at the answer. Even if she knew of a better team, she would never leave her friends. She'd been playing with some of them since kindergarten.

"My dad really thinks I need to keep focused on the future, and he thinks my old team is a bunch of losers. He said he won't even come and watch me until I find a better team."

"Well, is he coming this weekend?" Makena asked.

"Not unless we make it to the finals."

Wow, I hope we win so Skylar's dad will come, Makena thought. The girls arrived at the field, and Makena pointed to some of the players gathering by the far goal.

"Oh look!" Makena said, as they got closer. "Chloe's here."

"Who's Chloe?" Skylar asked.

"She's the girl on our team you are playing for."

"The dancer?" Skylar asked.

"She's not just a dancer. She's, like, kind of famous for her age."

Makena took off running toward her friend. "Chloe, hey!"

"Hey, Mac," Chloe said with a wave.

"I didn't know you were coming to practice," Makena said, excited. She'd hardly seen Chloe since school got out.

"My instructor got some sort of flu, so I was free and thought I would come play."

"Does that mean you can play this weekend?" Makena asked, hopeful.

"Nah," Chloe replied, "Unfortunately not. I'm a soloist in *Romeo and Juliet* in Central Park on Saturday. So lame."

Makena noticed Skylar staring at Chloe. Chloe got that a lot. Makena thought she was by far the prettiest girl in their school, tall and lean with long, super-straight, blond hair. Not only did she look like some kind of supermodel, she was sweet and probably the coolest girl Makena knew.

"This is Skylar," Makena said.

"Oh hey," Chloe said. "I've heard a lot about you."

Skylar gave a nod in reply.

"Girls, let's get started," Coach Lily called, and they all ran over to warm up.

They started with their regular stretching and then worked on technical skills, dribbling through and around small, neon-colored cones set up all over the field. Makena was amazed at Skylar's comfort with the ball; her first touch was incredible. It was like the ball was taped to her shoe.

"Isn't she awesome?" Makena whispered to Chloe during a water break.

"Yeah, she's really skilled," Chloe answered. Makena hoped her friend wasn't too bummed about missing another tournament.

"You're going to love playing with her," Makena said, hoping to cheer her up. "You know, in the fall."

"Yeah, for sure," Chloe said. "I can't wait."

Next, Coach Lily broke the girls into small-sided games meant to simulate situations they would face on the field. The first drill was one of Makena's favorites: four-versus-one keep-away in a small box grid she made with the cones. Makena was in the middle first and after a few passes was able to win the ball from Skylar. It was Skylar's turn to be in the middle and try to win the ball back from the girls passing it on the outside of the grid. Makena gave a pass to Chloe, but it was a little too slow, and Skylar was able to steal it off her foot.

"Oh, my bad pass, Chloe," Makena said. "Sorry!"

Chloe shrugged and smiled. Makena was so happy to have her at practice. She was always positive, and even if she wasn't the best player on the team, she was always fun.

"You're in the middle, dancer," Skylar said, and Makena could see Chloe's smile fade a little bit.

"Oh, it was my bad pass," Makena protested, moving into the circle.

"No, it's cool," Chloe said and took her turn in the middle.

On the outside, Makena, Skylar, Jessie, and Jasmine got on a roll, and Chloe fought to win the ball. Instead of getting set the way Lily taught them, she started lunging at the ball. Makena thought she looked frustrated.

"Oh, let's count how many passes we can get," Skylar said. "That's got to be, like, twelve."

Chloe was tired from chasing the ball around and slowed down. The fun little game didn't look very fun for Chloe anymore. Makena made a bad pass on purpose.

"Oh, I'm in," she said, wanting to give Chloe a break, but Coach Lily blew the whistle, and the drill was over.

"Girls, get some water."

"Where's Val?" Skylar asked during the break.

"Oh, she's in Texas. She'll be back in a few days."

"She's coming to the tournament, right?"

"Yeah, of course," Makena said.

"Awesome. She's a good player," Skylar said. "We need *her*."

Coach Lily came over to talk to the team.

"Girls, you know the deal this weekend. I expect perfect behavior from everyone. After our last tournament, I got an email that there was some incident at the hotel. They couldn't identify who the kids were, and I *know* it was none of you girls, but I want to remind you that when we go away and stay in hotels, we represent not only ourselves but our team, our club, our state, and, in this case, our country. Remember, this is a privilege and can be taken away."

Makena saw Skylar and Jessie smirking at one another.

"We clear on that?" Lily asked.

"Yes, Coach," Makena answered, a stab of guilt filling her stomach.

"OK, girls, we're going to have small-sided scrimmage for the rest of practice," Lily said as she started to hand out pinnies, the colorful bibs the girls wore in practice. "The rules of the game are as follows. There are no goals, so you want to try to keep possession of the ball. Every five passes will equal a goal. Practice keeping the ball. This is about possession."

"Practice makes perfect!" Chloe yelled.

"That's right," Lily said with a laugh. "OK, seven passes in a row equals two points. We'll play to three. Losers do push-ups, OK?"

This was another of Makena's favorites. She, Jessie, Jasmine, Kat, and Sydney put on blue bibs, while Skylar, Chloe, Ariana, Ella, and Tessa put on green bibs. Coach Lily put the ball in play.

The green team had a good run and, after five passes in a row, got a point. Makena and the blue team took over then and started working the ball around the field.

"Chloe, you need to mark tighter!" Skylar yelled.

Chloe sprinted toward Jessie, and Makena was actually happy when Chloe was able to intercept the pass. She gave the ball to Ariana. One pass. Two. Three. Four. Five. Six. Makena worked hard to win the ball back. One more pass, and the game was over. Chloe had the ball and looked around for someone to get open.

"Chloe, pass! We only need one more," Skylar yelled. "Pass! Now!"

Chloe picked her head up and made the pass. But Jasmine was too quick and intercepted the ball.

"What kind of pass was that?" Skylar muttered under her breath. Makena hoped that Chloe didn't hear her, but by the look on her face, it was clear that she had.

Practice ended a few minutes later, and instead of the normal fun chatter, the team was silent. Chloe drank from her water bottle quietly. Makena walked over to her.

"Hey, good luck with your performance this weekend. I hope it goes really well."

"Thanks" was all Chloe said. Makena wanted to say more, but the right words didn't come.

"We'll try to call you from Canada, OK?" Makena asked. "Me and Val."

Chloe nodded and walked away. "Good luck, Makena."

Makena was quiet as she and Skylar waited to cross the street, heading toward her dad's shop to get a snack. She was replaying some of the scenes from practice and thinking about Chloe. She hardly registered when a bus pulled up at the stop in front of them.

"I have *the best* idea," Skylar said. Grabbing Makena by the arm, she dragged her to the open bus door.

"This the bus to New York City?" Skylar asked the driver, who raised a tired finger to the electronic sign above her head, which read: *EXPRESS/MIDTOWN.*

"Perfect," Skylar said, fishing in her pocket. She pulled out a yellow MetroCard. "I'll pay for both of us."

"Skylar, what are you doing?" Makena asked in alarm as Skylar dragged her onto the bus.

"Oh, my dad got me the card. It's cool."

"No, I mean, where are we going? I thought we were just walking to town!"

"We said we were going to town; we didn't say *which* town. Come on, it'll be fun," Skylar answered, bolting to the back of the bus. The doors shut behind Makena while she was still in the stairwell.

Makena followed Skylar and said in a low voice, "Skylar, my mom doesn't let me go to New York City by myself. She's going to freak."

"She's not even going to know," Skylar said, stretching out on the seats. "I know where this bus stops. There's a supercool arcade right there. We'll go, check it out, and come back in a few hours, and no one will even know."

Makena looked out the grimy bus window. The scenery was changing quickly as they traveled south from Westchester. Apartment buildings and industrial shops replaced leafy trees. It was too late for her to get off now. Anyway, she had no idea how to get home. She did know that the West Side was about half an hour away. She looked at her phone. It was two thirty. As long as she was home by four thirty, her mom wouldn't worry. So if they

ANDREA MONTALBANO

hung out for an hour and got right back on the bus, they
could be home long before Makena's mom even noticed
they were gone.

The arcade was right where Skylar said it would be.
Makena started to relax a little. Using the ten-dollar bill
she'd brought, she bought eight dollars' worth of tokens,
played Space Duel, Dragon's Lair, and Moon Patrol, and
had a long battle of air hockey with Skylar. The girls used
the last two dollars for an ice cream sandwich and headed
back to the bus stop.

Makena's phone began to vibrate in her pocket. She
looked at the screen.

MOM CELL.

A taxi blared its horn at a passing fire truck. Makena
had to cover her ears to block the siren. She went to answer
the call.

"No! Don't," Skylar said and hit the Ignore button on
the phone. "She'll hear all the sirens and horns and know
where we are. Just text her."

"If I text her, she'll just keep calling. She's not much
of a texter."

"Well, whatever you do, don't answer now."

Makena knew Skylar was right but felt terrible not
picking up her mother's call. The phone vibrated again.

"Leave it," Skylar warned. "Wait until we get back to Brookville. Even the bus will be too obvious."

The bus to Brookville pulled up as if on cue. Makena sighed and looked at her phone's clock. It was nearly five o'clock. With any luck, they'd be home by five fifty. The phone buzzed again, and Makena could feel her mother's worry vibrating through the little machine. Skylar reached over and turned it off.

"We'll be back soon. No one's going to know. We're not going to get caught, Makena."

The ride to Midtown had taken about twenty-five minutes, but the journey home was more like two hours. The bus crawled along, slowed down by an accident on the highway. Skylar said she would handle everything with Makena's parents, but all Makena cared about was getting home and making sure her mother wasn't a total mess.

They leapt off the bus at close to six thirty and sprinted the distance to the Walsh home. Will was outside on his skateboard, the early summer sun extending twilight. He gave Makena a grave look as she and Skylar ran down the street.

"She's home!" Makena heard her brother yell. Seconds later, Makena's mother burst through the front door.

"Mac!" Her mother ran down the steps. "Where have

you been? I've been calling you for hours. Your father said you didn't come in after practice. He's driving all over town looking for you. I've been worried out of my mind and was about to call the police!"

Her mother grabbed Makena into a tight hug. When she pulled back, Makena saw tears in her eyes.

"Mom, we're fine. Really," Makena said weakly.

Skylar kicked right into apology. "Oh, Mrs. Walsh, this is all my fault. We went to town, but then we were horsing around behind the school, where we maybe shouldn't have been, and by mistake, I knocked Makena's phone out of her hand and down a gutter. Luckily, it didn't fall into any water, but we couldn't reach it. We could hear it ringing too, and Makena was dying to answer it, but it took so long for us to get it out. It's all my fault. I should have been more careful."

"So you guys were at the school this entire time?"

"Yeah, we tried everything to get the phone out. Makena told me how important it was to her. We didn't want to come home without it," Skylar lied easily.

"Why didn't you just use her phone?" Will asked, pointing at Skylar.

"I forgot to charge it last night. Battery's dead," Skylar answered without missing a beat.

Makena's mom looked at Skylar for a long minute and then turned to Makena. "This true?" she asked her daughter.

Makena hated lying to her mother, but she didn't know where the truth was hiding anymore. She nodded and picked at her cuticle, unable to meet her mother's gaze.

"Did you get my comic book at least?" Will asked, a knowing look on his face.

"Oh. No," Makena said, finally happy to tell the truth. "I totally forgot."

9

"Mom, Will's not helping," Makena complained, carrying another pile of clothes down the stairs.

"Oh, he's too involved with that comic book you got him. That was nice of you," her mom said. Makena glanced at her brother, who was curled up on the living room couch. Makena had gone with her father to get the *Asterix* comic book for Will after dropping Skylar off at the bus stop, and Will hadn't put it down since.

"You and I can handle this." Makena's mom gave her a smile.

"Where should I put these?" Makena asked, looking around the cramped, makeshift bedroom.

"I don't know. I'm still not sure how to make this work," Makena's mom said, frustration tingeing her voice.

Makena and her mother had been trying all morning

to fix up the small den off the living room for Papa. The room was tiny. There was only enough space for a narrow twin bed, an old dresser, a nightstand, and a small oxygen tank. Most of the den's original contents were now jammed into a corner of the basement.

"Why are we doing this again?" Makena asked.

"The doctors say going up and down the stairs is too hard on your grandfather's lungs."

"Why?"

"Well, he's not getting enough oxygen, and it makes him short of breath."

Makena stared at the oxygen tank. This was new. It looked like a fire extinguisher, except instead of a big black blaster, there was a thin, clear tube with two little attachments Papa put in his nose. Her grandfather had started using it several times a day. He didn't like it at all. Mostly because lack of oxygen had done nothing to cause him any lack of appetite. Papa was still obsessed with food and didn't appreciate little plastic things up his nose getting between him and his *antipasti*.

"What's it called again? In his lungs?" Makena asked.

"Emphysema."

"That doesn't sound good," Makena said.

"No, it's not good, but it could have been a lot worse.

We didn't know for a while, and that's why he had to see all those doctors." Makena's mom picked up a picture and dusted it off.

"Here, this might make it look homier."

Makena peered at the snapshot. The faded photo had been sitting on the dresser in her room for the past few months, but she'd never bothered to look at it. The image was of a young couple: a woman dressed in a winter coat standing next to a handsome young man wearing a hat. The woman held a baby. The Statue of Liberty rose in the background, green and grainy.

"Who is that?" Makena asked.

"That's me," her mom answered.

"Where?"

"I'm the baby. Wrapped up in a blanket. That's your Nanna, and that's Papa. I must have been just a few months old."

"Wow," Makena said, looking closely at the faces in the photo. It was hard to imagine the smiling young couple as her grandparents. She didn't remember her grandmother, who had died when Makena was four. Sometimes Makena forgot that Papa wasn't just her grandfather; he was also her mother's father. Makena would hate to see her own father not getting enough oxygen.

Makena felt an unpleasant knot tying itself up in her chest. Like when Will sat on her after she hid the remote. It made her feel awful inside.

"Look on the bright side, Mac. You can have your room back now," her mom said and managed a small smile. She left to go get the rest of Papa's clothes.

Makena sat on the bed, holding the picture and feeling as small as the images in the frame. She felt so guilty for lying to her mother but couldn't bring herself to tell her about all of Skylar's lies. Makena wanted to confess, but her mom was so preoccupied with Papa that she didn't want to make things worse.

She sat on the bed, looking at the picture. On cue, Papa shuffled in.

"Where's the lunch? Where's your mother?" he asked Makena in his thick Italian accent. Papa had come to the United States from Sicily when he was a teenager.

Makena smiled at the old man. No amount of emphysema was going to keep Papa from food.

"She's upstairs," Makena answered. "I can make you something to eat."

"*Tu?*" Papa said with a laugh. He clapped his hands in front of himself and looked at Makena like she couldn't even open a can of soup. "*Ma, sei pazza.*"

"I'm not crazy! I can cook, you know," Makena said. "Dad taught me."

Makena's grandfather laughed, but the laugh quickly turned into a cough, a deep hacking cough that made him double over. The sound made Makena feel short of breath. Papa gestured to Makena to help; she jumped up, walked him to the bed, and hooked him up to the oxygen.

The coughing subsided after a few minutes. Makena sat quietly next to Papa. He put his hand over hers.

Makena's mom came into the den with an armful of clothes. Seeing her father hooked up to his oxygen tank, she asked, "What happened?"

"I told Papa I would make him lunch, and he laughed so hard he needed help breathing."

Makena's mom smiled at her dad. "She's not half bad," her mom said. Papa gestured with both hands, fingers to thumbs, which needed no translation. He wasn't buying it.

Makena had dropped the framed photo when she got up to help him. Now she picked it up and put it back on the nightstand, hoping Papa would like seeing it there.

Instead, he became very upset. Grabbing the picture, his eyes narrowed and he blurted in rapid-fire Italian, "*Ma guarda! Ecco la causa di tutti i miei problemi. Hai visto? 'Na sigaretta in mano anche li.*"

Makena had no idea what was going on. She knew some Italian, but that was too fast.

"What'd he say? What'd he say?" Makena asked, worried that she'd upset him.

"He said…he can see the cause of all his problems," Makena's mother replied.

Papa pointed to the image. "*Guarda bene*," he said.

Makena knew that meant *look carefully*. She peered closely at the image.

"I know, that's Mom in the blanket," she said.

"No," her grandfather replied. "Here."

He was pointing at himself in the photo. Finally, Makena saw it. There was a small white cigarette in Papa's hand; a swirl of smoke shadowed the young family. Makena had never seen her grandfather smoke anything in her life.

"I never knew you smoked, Papa." Makena said. "That's gross."

Papa nodded. "*Sì.*"

10

"Dad, what time are they coming again?" Makena asked.

"Six o'clock."

"What time is it now?"

"It's, uh, five fifty-nine, approximately five minutes since you last asked me the time at five fifty-four." Makena's dad looked up from his watch with a mixture of exhaustion and amusement. He was adding charcoal to the grill on the small patio next to the family's house.

"What's for dinner again?"

"Oh, it's a surprise from Miguel. We're going to try out some recipes he brought back from his sister in Texas, *frijoles charros* and some *chiles rellenos*."

Makena had no idea what any of that was, but her mouth still watered at the thought. Everything her father made was delicious, and although she could never tell her dad, everything that Miguel, Val's father, made was even better. It was *ultra*-delicious. Putting the two of them together was bound to be good. Makena watched her dad carefully arrange his ingredients on the small table next to the grill, like he was setting up a chessboard. Her stomach growled with hunger—and nervousness. She was anxious to see Val, who had been away visiting relatives for almost two weeks.

Makena turned back to her brother. After their thumb war had turned too violent, their father had decreed a non-contact waiting game in order. So now they were sitting at the worn wooden picnic table in the backyard playing finger football. The score was tied at 27 to 27, and Will was kicking an extra point. If he could flick the little paper triangle through the goalpost Makena made by holding her thumbs together, fingers up, he would win the Paper Football Super Bowl. The loser had to set and clear the table, so stakes were high.

"You've got one more minute, Will. Take your best shot."

"No moving," Will said, eyeing his sister from across the table. He got eye level with the stadium field/picnic table. It was do-or-die. He balanced the paper triangle "ball" with his finger and prepared to kick it by flicking it with his forefinger.

"Clock's ticking. Tick. Tock," Makena said, trying to psych him out.

"Hold on," Will said, sitting up suddenly. "The ball's falling apart. Time-out."

"There are no time-outs," Makena said.

"Yes, you get three time-outs."

"OK, thirty seconds. Go." Makena looked around the corner for any sign of Miguel and Val.

Will opened the triangle. The ball was simple enough to make, a piece of lined paper folded into a long strip and then folded up diagonally with the end of the strip tucked into the last fold. Definitely not high-tech.

Makena thought she heard a car door.

"That them?" she asked her dad, who had a view of the driveway.

"No, Mac, not yet."

Makena looked back at her brother and saw that he had unfolded the entire ball.

"Your time is up. What are you doing?" she asked. Then she noticed some familiar writing on the paper.

Makena jumped up from her seat. "Give that to me!"

"No, it's my shot!"

She mustered her sweetest tone. "Please, can I have it, Will?"

"Then you forfeit," Will said, holding the paper behind him.

"Fine, I forfeit. You win," Makena replied.

A car door slammed in the driveway.

"They're here!" Will yelled, jumping up from the table and tossing the paper into the air. Makena scrambled to catch it before it hit the ground.

The blue paper had folds and creases all through it. Makena put it onto the table and tried to straighten it out as best she could. She could hear Val and Miguel greeting Will in the driveway. Makena wanted to run to meet her friend, but something kept her glued to the paper for an extra minute. At the top of the page were the words SOCCER SISTERS in bubble letters and a few lines underneath.

She realized she must have left it lying around. Makena had been thinking about her team and doodling little Soccer Sisters pictures. Her favorite was of a girl kicking a ball that turned into a heart.

"Mac!" the unmistakable voice of her best friend called.

"Howdy, pardner! How was Texas?" Makena asked with a drawl. She took the paper and stuffed it into the elastic waistband of her shorts. Val plopped down on the bench looking tanned and happy.

"Hot," she announced.

"What did you do with your cousins?" Makena asked.

"Well, we hung out. Played a lot of soccer. Rode some horses. Went swimming. Like I said, it was super hot. Oh, and we found this." Val casually tossed a small plastic bag onto the table.

"What is it?" Makena asked, picking up the bag.

"A scorpion."

Makena dropped the bag with a yelp. "Val!"

"It's dead, don't worry. I found it under my bed," Val said. "I brought it back to show your mom. Figured she'd know everything about it."

"That's just wrong," Makena said, trying to imagine sleeping above a deadly scorpion.

"No way! That's awesome!" Will yelled. "Can I show Mom?"

"Sure, that's why I brought it," Val answered with a grin. Will snatched up the bag and ran into the house.

"So what did you get up to?" Val asked. "Did you get your phone finally?"

"Yeah, I got my phone," Makena answered softly.

"Huh. I thought you'd be happier," Val said. She knew Makena had been begging for one.

"No, I'm happy." Makena took the folded paper into her hand and held it under the table.

"Is that it? Can I see it?" Val asked.

"Oh, this is just a piece of paper," Makena answered quickly. "But, Val?"

"That's me," Val answered with a puzzled look.

Makena took a deep breath. "I've got to tell you something. Skylar came to stay for a few days."

"Skylar?" Val asked, surprised. "Why did she come here?"

"We had a little pre-tournament practice, and she stayed over."

Val didn't say anything. Makena's fingers fiddled with the paper. She took another deep breath.

"Val?"

"Mac, just spit it out already."

The words were hard to get out, but once the weeks of pent-up lies and secrets started flowing, they spilled from Makena's lips like cars going down a roller coaster.

"Skylar came to visit, and she was so mean to Chloe at practice, and then we took the bus to the city and went to an arcade, and then we lied to my mom's face about it. And remember the last game of the tournament? Me, Jessie, and Skylar snuck out and went to the hot tub, which was awesome, but then it wasn't awesome because the security guards busted us, and we ran away, and Skylar stole a golf cart and crashed it, and we didn't get any sleep, and I was so tired I played the worst game of my life, and we lost, but we didn't get caught, and Skylar says if you don't get caught, it's not a crime, but I feel so awful inside. I had to tell you, and I know you're going to hate me, but…"

"Breathe," Val said, holding up her hand to stop her friend.

Makena took a deep breath. Tears welled up in her eyes. She stared at Val, whose eyes had opened wide.

Val sighed. Makena braced herself.

Finally, Val spoke, "First of all, I would never hate you."

Makena looked up at her, feeling the knot in her stomach loosen just a little.

"But." Val paused and then launched into her own flood of words. "What the heck is the matter with you? You went without me? Why can't you just say no? Don't you know how to do that? Did you forget?"

"I don't know," Makena said quietly.

"Why do you always do what she says?" Val asked. "That's just not like you."

"I guess she's just exciting and I went along with her. Plus she knows so much about soccer," Makena said.

"Well, she knows a lot about cheap soccer," Val replied. "Not my style."

Makena squeezed the paper in her hand, and it made a sound.

"What is that?"

Makena brought the paper up. "Oh, I was thinking about our team."

"Can I see it?" Val asked, unfurling the paper.

Makena handed over the paper. It was already pretty well worn. Next to the *Soccer Sisters*, she had drawn a couple of pictures of hearts and soccer balls. She had also written a few words down: *Team*, *Fun*, *Sportsmanship*, and the names of her teammates.

"I like the picture of the girl when she kicks the ball the best," Val said.

"Thanks. I was thinking of coming up with, you know, some kind of rules, like when you make a club?"

"For our team?" Val asked. "That might be cool. What do you have so far?"

"Not much."

"Well, I would definitely vote for one about sportsmanship. I really don't like that cheap stuff Skylar pulls all the time."

Makena immediately thought back to Skylar's fake ankle injury. As usual, Val was right. That's not what their team was about.

"Sportsmanship. OK, for sure," Makena said. "Hang on, I need a pen."

As Makena got up to run into the house, she stopped short and gave Val a tight hug. She felt so relieved to have finally told her everything.

"What am I going to do?" Makena asked.

"What do you mean?"

"I mean, in Canada and at practice this week. When Skylar's there. What am I going to do?"

"First of all, you're going to practice saying no. Second, you're going to remember that this is our team, not Skylar's."

Val grabbed the blue piece of paper and waved it around.

Makena and Val talked about the tournament until dinner was ready. They stuffed themselves with Miguel's *ultra*-deliciousness. As they ate, Makena's mom taught them about scorpions. They learned that there are almost two thousand scorpion species, and thirty or forty have strong enough poison to kill a person. Apparently people in China liked to eat them fried with a mound of ants, but you had to take out the stingers first.

Makena and Val decided to stick with frijoles.

11

Two days later, Makena and Val were happily squashed in the back of the Walshs' minivan, bookending a duffel bag, with soccer balls at their feet and family luggage looming behind. They were headed to the Roberts Cup in Toronto, Ontario.

Makena still couldn't believe that her mother, father, brother, grandfather, and best friend were taking a road trip together. This was a first. But here they were: Papa snoring like a machine gun in the second row, Will doing battle on his Nintendo 3DS, and her parents giggling in the front seat like they were on a date. The minivan hummed along, long stretches of highway floating by like blurry postcard pictures.

Val and Makena spent most of the drive plotting soccer strategy and looking at a picture book about Canada, a gift from Val's father, who was watching the shop so Makena's dad could make the trip. Papa's doctors had given the green light as long as he didn't walk too far, so there was also a wheelchair strapped to the roof of the van. After the tournament, they were driving over to see Niagara Falls. Apparently Papa had always wanted to visit and had heard hot dogs were cheaper north of the border.

"Why so quiet?" Val asked after a long silence.

"Just thinking," Makena said.

"About?" Val asked.

"Oh, you know. *Everything*," Makena said.

Val nodded. She knew she couldn't say anything out loud about "everything," so she lowered her voice and whispered with a smile, "I got your back."

In Canada, the Breakers started off with a bang, playing their first game against a team from New Hampshire called the Firecrackers. They were duds. The Breakers easily went up 2 to 0 by halftime; the final score was 4 to 0. Val had two goals, and Jessie and Skylar scored the other two. Makena didn't score but assisted on the last two goals.

Makena was doing her best to ignore Skylar and focus on soccer. Luckily, the night before the first game, Makena and Val stayed with Makena's family on the road, arriving just in time to play. But tonight Makena, Val, Jessie, and

Skylar were sharing a room at the hotel where the rest of the team was staying. Makena was nervous but determined to keep her distance.

During the breaks, Makena made sure to sit with all her Soccer Sisters at a big table. At one point, Skylar wanted to talk about their New York City adventure, but Makena changed the subject.

Skylar finally cornered Makena during warm-up for the second game.

"Man, you have got to see how awesome our hotel is! We stayed there last night. It has an indoor pool on the top floor, a pool table, and a huge TV room. We have to check it out tonight. You know, late night," Skylar whispered.

Makena was tying her shoe and looked around for Val for support.

"Makena, you in?"

"Not this time, Skylar," Makena said.

"Why not? It'll be crazy," Skylar said.

"Skylar, I'm just here to play in the tournament and be with my family. That's all I'm doing this weekend."

Makena grabbed her ball and started to move away.

"Hey, wait a minute…" Skylar called after her, but Makena kept moving. Then she decided it was time she had to face Skylar and stopped.

"Skylar, look, you are a great player, and we've had some fun times, but I just don't want to get in trouble again. I'm trying to think about my team. I'm not going to turn you in or anything, but sorry, I'm just not going to sneak out again. OK?"

Skylar stared at her but didn't reply, so Makena just shrugged and kept walking.

The second game was a lot tighter. It was against a tough team from Michigan called the Wolfpack. Neither side had much success scoring, but there were close calls for both teams. During the final minutes of the game, Makena took a pass from Skylar by the end line. It was a hard, flat delivery, and a Wolfpack defender lunged to intercept. She got her foot in, and the ball deflected off Makena's shin and out of bounds. The linesperson raised his flag and pointed to the corner.

The referee had been behind the play and had also missed the deflection off Makena's leg.

Skylar didn't wait.

"Corner kick!" she yelled, running over to grab the ball.

A corner kick was an awesome scoring opportunity, and Makena knew it. The Breakers needed a goal badly. All she had to do was let Skylar kick it in.

Instead, Makena turned and said, "Referee, the

ball hit my leg before it went out. It's a goal kick. It's their ball."

"Thanks, number eight," the referee replied, pulling out her pen to write something down on the little pad in her front pocket. Makena hoped she wasn't in trouble.

"Goal kick!" the referee called, blowing her whistle.

"But, Ref, the linesman said it was a corner kick!" Skylar cried, running toward the corner flag with the ball.

"Skylar, it hit my leg. It's a goal kick," Makena said, turning and jogging upfield to get in position.

"Number six, drop the ball. Next time you open your mouth, it's a yellow," the referee said to Skylar.

Skylar didn't open her mouth, but she did purposely throw the ball to the corner of the field. The referee immediately blew her whistle and took a yellow card out of her pocket. She called Skylar over and held the card up in the air, writing another note in the little book.

Coach Lily immediately called for a substitution and pulled Skylar off the field. Makena watched Skylar sulk to the sidelines, glaring at her.

Coach Lily kept Skylar on the bench for the rest of the game. In the final minutes, Makena and Val connected with a give-and-go outside the box. Val fired one of her trademark screamers into the upper corner.

1 to 0 Breakers.

But the Wolfpack kept up the pressure and the Breakers buckled down. Their coach yelled to collapse the defense. They only had to hold on for another minute or so.

In the team's last attack, a Wolfpack defender made a beautiful run down the line. The girl was incredibly fast, with long, blond hair that reminded Makena of Brandi Chastain, one of her all-time favorite players. Val tracked the defender down the line and managed to corner her near the sideline. Makena moved in to help just as the ball popped loose and Val went in for a tackle.

The next few seconds unfolded in slow motion. Val lunged forward with her right leg and managed to poke the ball as she slid on the ground. The Wolfpack defender was taken by surprise but moved forward, driving the ball forward with her stomach. Val got up quickly and turned to follow but suddenly cried out and crumpled to the ground.

Val Flores was the toughest player Makena had ever seen. She was brave beyond words. She was strong. Val never went down.

Val was down and staying down.

Makena didn't even know where the ball was. She rushed over to her friend. Val was holding her knee, crying.

"Val! What happened?"

"I don't know," Val managed to say through her tears. "When I turned, I felt something happen to my knee."

Makena heard the referee's whistle. In an instant, Coach Lily and then Makena's parents were by their side on the ground, helping Val.

Parents are not allowed on the field during a game, even for an injury. Makena looked around, confused.

"Mom, Val's hurt. But you have to wait until the game's over."

"The game is over," her mom answered. "You won. I think you just didn't notice."

Makena looked up and saw that the two teams were solemnly shaking hands. Val's injury must have happened in the very last seconds of the game.

Makena didn't care. She was only worried about her friend.

12

"Look on the bright side," Makena said. "At least you got a free ride in Papa's wheelchair."

"Great" was the only reply from a very depressed Val.

They were sitting together on a long wooden bench in the medical tent, waiting for someone to bring Val a pair of crutches. Val's knee was wrapped in ice and propped up on Makena's leg. Makena was a little numb from sitting in the same position for so long, but she was afraid that moving would hurt Val. Val was being her brave self, but Makena could tell she was in a lot of pain.

There had been quite a few injuries that day, including one concussion, so it was well into the evening by the time the doctor finally saw Val. Makena's parents stayed as long as they could, but they finally had to take Papa and Will back to the hotel. Coach Lily was outside talking with an important-looking man.

Before he left, the doctor told Val she would probably need to get a test called an MRI to check her ligaments for damage, but that would have to be back in New York.

The tent flap opened. Makena felt the chill from the night air.

"How you girls doing?" A tall man with a beard and glasses approached Makena and Val. He carried a pair of metal crutches.

"We're OK," Makena answered. Val was quiet.

"I'm Mr. Hardin. I'm the director of the Roberts Cup," he said in a very kind voice, sitting down next to Val and Makena. "We're sure sorry that you hurt your knee today, Val. Here are some crutches that you can use. Your coach has the report from the doctor. Looks like it might just be a sprain, but you'll need to get yourself checked by your own doctor in a few days. Do you understand?"

"Yes," Val answered. "Thank you."

"You're welcome. I spoke with your father, and I know your coach has too. Make sure someone gets that report to your dad."

"I'm sure my parents will take care of it," Makena said. "We're BFFs."

"You're what?"

"We're best friends forever."

"Ah, of course. What's your name?" Mr. Hardin asked.

"I'm Makena Walsh."

"Nice to meet you, Makena." Mr. Hardin looked at Makena and Val with a droll smile. "You girls sure look like you could use a shower and some dinner."

"I could eat ten cheeseburgers," Val answered.

"Maybe twenty," Makena said.

"How long have you been here?" he asked.

"We have no idea," Makena answered.

"Forever," Val said at the same time.

"You sat with her the whole time?" Mr. Hardin asked Makena.

"Of course," Makena said, adjusting Val's ice pack as it slipped to the side. "We never give up on one another. We're Soccer Sisters."

13

Makena and Val didn't make it back to the hotel until close to ten. Lily took them through the drive-through of a burger joint so Val didn't have to walk around. Val said her knee was starting to feel a little better, but she still couldn't put any pressure on it or walk. Makena and Val inhaled about six sliders each with a milk shake and fries. Now they were ready to fall straight into bed.

Makena still had to play in the championship game at noon the next day, but Val was out for a while. Coach Lily gave them the key to Room 314, said she'd see them in the lobby for breakfast, and told them to try to get some rest.

All Makena wanted to do was take a shower, help Val get settled, and dive into a nice, clean bed. After two games and sitting in the medical tent, Makena was exhausted.

Makena turned the key quietly and cracked open the door, hoping for sleeping girls and silence. Instead, Skylar and Jessie were watching TV and tossing a soccer ball between the two beds.

"Man, what took you guys so long?" Skylar asked.

Makena answered, "We've been sitting in the medical tent."

"It didn't look like much of an injury, that's all," Skylar said.

Val didn't bother to reply. She just crutched her way to the bathroom and shut the door. Makena heard the shower water start.

"I'm tired. Which is my bed?" she asked Jessie and Skylar.

"Oh, we've been hanging out in both. Whichever one you want," Jessie said.

Makena picked the bed closest to the bathroom to make it easier for Val.

"We'll sleep here."

"You guys totally missed out," Skylar said, throwing the ball up in the air and catching it. "We were swimming in the pool for, like, hours. It was awesome."

"Sounds great," Makena said, fishing her pajamas out of her luggage. She didn't want to talk about pools or hot tubs. All she could think about was Val and the fact that she couldn't play in the morning.

"It *was* great. We're going back later," Skylar said.

Makena didn't respond. *Hurry up, Val*, she thought. She just wanted to get into the shower and away from Skylar.

"Did you hear me?" Skylar asked. "We're going back later."

"Don't you think you should rest before the game?" Makena said.

"We've been sitting around all night, waiting for you," Skylar answered.

"You shouldn't be waiting for me. I told you I'm not going out again. We have a huge game tomorrow."

"Yeah, well, we almost didn't," Skylar said to Makena.

"What's that supposed to mean?" Makena asked.

"You almost gave the game away. You gave away a corner kick, and you made me get a yellow," Skylar said, moving in a little closer.

"I didn't get you a yellow card. You did that on your own."

"You gave away a corner kick," Skylar said. "That was stupid."

"No, I didn't. I just didn't lie about it. The ball hit me and went out. It was a goal kick. I think I know what a goal kick is." Makena just wanted the conversation to be over.

"Oh, whatev," Skylar said, grabbing the remote and flopping on the other bed.

Val emerged from the bathroom and got right into her bed.

"So, let's go," Skylar said quietly to Makena.

"Go where?" Makena moved toward the bathroom.

"To the pool. They have a shower there. I said… let's go."

Makena took a deep breath. She could feel Val watching her from the bed.

"Skylar, no. I'm not going anywhere but to bed. We have a huge game tomorrow, and I want to play my best. I told you I am not leaving this room."

Makena got up and went into the steamy bathroom. As she closed the door, she heard Skylar say under her breath, "Wanna bet?"

14

It wasn't just the siren that woke Makena. It was the pounding on the door.

"Girls! Get up!" Jasmine's mother was in motion. "Get up! We have to evacuate!" There was nothing singsongy about her voice, and it got Makena, Jessie, and Val moving quickly.

Fire alarm sirens blasted through the hallway. Automated recordings in English and French kept repeating, "The fire alarm has been activated. Do not use the elevators. Use the stairs and gather in the lobby. This is not a test."

Makena helped Val grab her crutches and hobble down the hallway. Lights blinked in little boxes on the walls, leading them to the stairs.

"Where's Skylar?" Makena asked Jessie. Makena had seen Skylar in bed asleep, or what looked like sleep, when she got out of the shower. She wasn't with them now though.

"I don't know," Jessie answered, holding the door to the stairs open for Val. "Maybe she's in the pool? It's on the top floor."

Val soldiered down the first flight of stairs with her crutches but nearly fell at the top of the second landing. The crutches were too big for her small frame. For the rest of the trip down the stairs, Makena carried them and Val hopped on her good leg, using the railing for support. She didn't complain the entire way down, but Makena knew it must have hurt.

When they were nearly at the lobby, Makena heard a familiar, welcoming voice. Her mother, her father, and Will were helping Papa down the stairs right behind them. Their room was on the sixth floor.

"Oh, Mac, there you are. What a relief. Your father was about to go make sure you were OK." At the sight of Val hopping, Makena's mom's brow crinkled. "Poor Val. How are you managing?"

"I'm fine, Mrs. W," Val answered. "I'm a good hopper."

"You're a good egg is what you are," Makena's mom said.

Makena saw that Papa was moving slowly with help from Will and her father. She stepped up to help.

"Where's his oxygen?" she asked.

"There was no time," her father answered. "The fire marshal said we had to go."

"I can go back and get it," Makena said.

"*No!*" Papa yelled.

"OK, Papa," Makena answered.

They made it to the lobby in a group and joined a mass of bleary-eyed hotel guests, most of whom were wearing matching hotel bathrobes. They looked like some kind of giant sleepover party, except that no one was giggling or braiding hair. Everyone had the same startled yet groggy look of concern and irritation at having been rudely awakened by the blare of a fire alarm bell.

"Is there really a fire, Mom?" Will asked.

"I'm not sure yet," Mrs. Walsh answered. "But fire alarms don't usually go off in the middle of the night for no reason. We'll have to wait until they check the hotel. For your grandfather's sake, I hope it isn't too long."

Papa had taken a seat on one of the lobby sofas. Makena, Val, and Jessie huddled together with him.

Makena saw Lily jogging across the lobby.

"Nine, ten, eleven..." Lily said. "I'm missing one. I need twelve players."

Lily frantically scanned the lobby. Another group of Breakers was gathered with Jasmine's mom on a second couch. But Makena knew who was missing.

"Coach Lily, Skylar's not here," she said.

"What? Where is she? Didn't she come down with you three?"

Before Makena could say no, Skylar came running out of the stairwell, breathing hard.

"Twelve. Phew," Lily said when he saw Skylar, relief visible on her face.

"Oh, there's Skylar," Makena's mom said. "Honey, what took you so long?"

"Oh, well, I was…" Skylar paused to catch her breath. "After I assisted my teammates to safety, I went back up to help some of the elderly hotel guests on the stairs. I'm so sorry if I caused anyone to worry."

Makena opened her mouth to tell Lily and her mother that Skylar was lying. Skylar hadn't helped any of her teammates, and Makena was sure she hadn't been helping any elderly guests either.

"Coach!" Makena called, but she didn't hear her because at that moment the hotel manager's booming, French-accented voice filled the lobby.

"Ladies and gentlemen, please forgive this extraordinary inconvenience. The fire marshal has just informed me there is no fire. The hotel is safe. A fire alarm was triggered in the upstairs pool area. We are currently investigating.

We apologize for the disruption, but your safety is of the utmost importance. Thank you for your cooperation. You may return to your rooms. Please allow those with small children or the elderly access to the elevators first. We hope you will all join us in the solarium dining hall tomorrow for a complimentary continental breakfast. Again, thank you for your cooperation, and good night."

By the time the hotel manager started to repeat the announcement in French, most of the guests were already on their way back to their rooms. Lily told the Breakers that they should take the stairs. Papa was offered the first elevator car by the hotel manager, and Makena walked with him, holding his arm to support him.

"*Grazie, cara,*" he said as they moved slowly toward the elevator bank.

"Mac, you can go on up with your grandfather," Coach Lily called after her.

Skylar followed them to the elevator and held the doors open for Makena and her family.

As the elevator continued to fill with guests, Makena moved to the back. The doors were closing when Skylar moved forward and whispered to Makena, "Told ya."

15

Makena got back to the room as quickly as she could. She knocked loudly on the door, and Jessie answered.

"Hey, Mac," she said. "How's your grandfather?"

"He's fine," Makena answered, pushing past her. "Where's Skylar?"

"Looking for me?" a voice said. Skylar was perched on her bed, a smug smile on her face.

"You did this," Makena accused, pointing at Skylar.

"Wasn't that awesome? Did you see all those old farts hobbling around in matching robes? I nearly peed my pants laughing," Skylar said. "Oh, and that French manager guy with the crazy accent? That was the best part."

"Wait a minute," Val interrupted. "Skylar, you pulled the fire alarm?"

Makena nodded. "Of course she did."

"Dude!" Val said, sitting up in bed. "Are you serious?"

"Oh, come on. It was easy. I saw the box up next to the lifeguard's chair. Piece of cake. The only problem was it turns off the elevators. I didn't know that, so I had to run all the way down. Man, I'm tired. That was the only bummer."

"Only bummer? Skylar! One of those old geezers was my grandfather. You know? Papa? He had to walk down six flights of stairs and didn't even have time to get his oxygen tank."

Skylar shrugged. "He seemed OK when I saw him."

"I nearly broke my neck hopping down the stairs," Val chimed in.

"You're fine too. Wow, you guys are annoying. I'm going to sleep," Skylar said.

"You don't even care, do you? You don't get it," Makena said.

"Not really. And I don't know what you're getting all worked up about, Makena. You're the one who snuck out last time."

"Yeah, I did. And you know what? I played the worst game of my life the next day. I missed a penalty kick. I lost the game for us! Sure, I snuck out, but I shouldn't have, and

I know that now. I also shouldn't have let you drag me off to Manhattan."

"Whoa. You guys went to New York City? Alone?" Jessie asked.

"Yeah, we took the bus to an arcade. It was great," Skylar said.

"It was not great!" Makena yelled. "You lied to my mom's face!"

"I got you out of trouble, so, yeah, you're welcome."

"You're welcome? Skylar, you can't just go around lying to people. You can't do that! It's wrong!"

"Remember, it's not a crime…"

"*It doesn't matter if you don't get caught! It's still wrong!*" Makena yelled, not caring if she woke up the entire hotel.

"OK, Makena," she heard Val say gently.

"I'm not going to let you get away with this, Skylar," Makena said firmly.

Skylar pulled the covers up to her shoulders. "I'm going to sleep, and you're not doing anything. You never do. You don't have the guts. Plus, if you turn me in, I'll tell Coach it was you who made me sneak out and you who took the golf cart. Oh, and I'm pretty sure your mom and dad would be interested to know about our little city adventure."

"I don't care if they find out," Makena said.

Skylar sat back up and glared at Makena. "Oh, yes, you do. You turn me in, we lose tomorrow. It's as simple as that. Val's out. Without you, me, and Jessie, we won't have enough players."

Makena saw Jessie nodding in agreement.

"She's right, Mac."

"If you turn me in," Skylar continued, "your precious Breakers will have to forfeit the championship. You care, but I don't. You know why? Because I'm not really one of your stupid Soccer Sisters anyway."

"No," Makena said as she headed for the door. "You're not."

16

The next morning, Makena wanted coffee for the first time in her life. She had to settle for the sip of Diet Coke her mom gave her on the way to the field. She didn't remember ever having been so exhausted. How was she going to make it through the day, much less the rest of the game?

The score was 2 to 2 by the middle of the second half. The Breakers were holding their own but fading fast because of their middle-of-the-night false alarm. They were playing a Canadian team called the Fury.

Fury would have also been an appropriate word for the scene in Makena's parents' hotel room the night before. Makena woke up her mother and father and spilled her guts about everything. She told them about the hot tub, the golf cart, sneaking into the city, and how Skylar had admitted to setting off the fire alarm.

Makena's father wanted to ground her for life. Makena was in so much trouble that her brother Will didn't even bother to gloat. Yet facing her mother was worse. Makena wished her mother had yelled at her. That would have been easier. But her mother said nothing when Makena confessed to lying to her face. She just stared at her daughter like she was seeing a stranger. The hurt in her mom's eyes crushed Makena. It was a punishment ten times worse than anything her father could come up with—which was saying something.

Makena shook the images from her head and moved for a throw-in, breaking free of a defender and calling for the ball. She was determined not to fall even one step behind. She would not let her team down again. But scenes from the last night still flashed in her mind constantly, even as she ran upfield with the ball at her feet.

"I'm packing right now," Makena's dad had said. "We're going home this second!"

In the end, it was Papa who rescued Makena.

"*Brava*," he said to the room. Then Papa told her parents that at least Makena had been brave enough to finally stand up for herself. He knew how hard that could be. Plus he was tired, he wasn't going anywhere, and he still wanted to eat hot dogs at the big waterfall.

Makena made a sharp pass out wide to Jasmine.

Jasmine brought the ball down to the goal line but missed the cross; the Fury were awarded a goal kick.

As Makena waited for the Fury player to get the ball, she looked at her teammates, all ready for action in their uniforms, a ponytail or braid on every head, a look of concentration teachers would have been thrilled to see in any classroom on every face.

The Soccer Sisters had voted that morning to play shorthanded. Or short-footed, as Mrs. Manikas put it. Makena's parents decided it wasn't fair to punish the whole team for her mistakes. Jessie's parents basically said the same thing when Coach Lily called them that morning, although Makena knew that Jessie was angry at her for turning her in.

Makena wondered if Skylar's parents had arrived to pick her up yet. Makena realized that Skylar's dad hadn't shown up to even the finals, which might have been why Skylar was acting out so much. As it turned out, the hotel's video cameras had captured the whole fire alarm escapade after all. Makena was grounded, but Skylar was in some real trouble.

Makena looked over to the strong Fury midfielder covering her. The whole Fury team spoke French to one another, but Makena knew her name was Ava. Ava had scored the game's first goal on a free kick, and she was sticking to Makena like glue.

The Fury goal kick was low; Makena trapped it on her thigh, moving forward into the box. As she made a move to her right to try to get a shot off, she was jostled from behind. Makena was right in front of the goal. She stumbled hard and saw the referee put his whistle to his mouth. Makena knew if she threw herself on the ground, she would probably be awarded a penalty kick. She heard Skylar's voice in her head.

Dive! Get the call!

Makena put her hand on the ground and caught her balance.

The referee yelled, "Play on!"

The Fury goalie picked up the ball and punted it upfield. Makena willed her legs to move back into defense. For some reason, she was running lighter now. She was moving faster. Soccer was clear to her again.

The field felt soft and familiar under her feet, and the hum of the fans and the coaches tickled her ears and inspired her. The weight of her confusion lifted. For the first time in a long time, Makena's mind felt free and soccer once again felt amazing.

Ava got the ball at midfield and made an attacking run down the middle. Jessie was out of position, so Makena gave chase. Ava had some serious moves. Makena kept close. As she approached the box, Ava went down with a yell. Makena knew she hadn't touched her. She didn't know why she'd fallen.

Yelping, Ava held her ankle and rolled back and forth. Makena stopped immediately and bent down to see if she was OK. The ball rolled out of bounds.

"Are you all right?" Makena asked.

"Yes, I'm OK," Ava said in English with a cute French accent. "I think I stepped in a hole."

Makena heard the referee blow the whistle and call for the coach and trainer. She offered her hand to the girl and Ava got up, brushing herself off. The referee waved the coach and trainer off and said, "Blue ball."

Makena ran over to take it, but it didn't feel like it should be her ball. If Ava hadn't stepped in a hole, it would still be the Fury's ball. Makena looked at Lily and she nodded, understanding what she wanted to do. She threw the ball to a Fury defender instead of one of her teammates.

The Fury moved the ball from defender to defender, and while the Breakers had a few chances, they failed to score. Finally, the Fury got the ball to their superstar Ava, who didn't miss the opportunity.

She hit the ball from outside the box, and with barely

even a spin, the ball knuckled its way past Ariana, the Breakers' goalie. The Fury exploded in celebration. The Breakers played their hearts out in the last few minutes, but the championship was over.

Fury 3, Breakers 2 was the final score.

"I want to go now, Mom," Makena said as she was greeted on the sideline with a tight hug.

"OK, honey," Makena's mom said. "I'm exhausted just watching you run so much. You played great, Makena. I was proud of you today."

"I'm sorry you came all this way to see me lose," Makena said.

Makena's mom bent down so that they were at eye level. "I came all this way to see you shine."

Makena and the Breakers gathered up their bags and balls and headed slowly for the cars. Lily and the other parents ruffled Makena's hair and congratulated her on how well she'd played. Even Mr. Hardin, the tournament director, made a point of finding Makena after the game and reminding her, "Don't leave without your medals."

"Oh, Mom, I don't care about any medals today."

"We'll go right after the little ceremony."

Both teams gathered around a makeshift podium,

which was really a table by the parking lot. A box on top was filled with trophies for the winners and silver medals for the runners-up. Makena leaned against her mother, watching Ava and her teammates stare excitedly at the prizes.

Mr. Hardin stepped to the table and said in his booming voice, "Girls, it's been quite a weekend. We have a few awards to present, so let's get started."

He nodded to an assistant, who gathered up the medals.

"First, to the Brookville Breakers, for a game well played. We thank you for coming all the way to Canada for this exciting event."

There were polite claps all around as the girls moved forward one by one. The assistant placed a thick red ribbon around each player's neck. The girls looked forlornly at their second-place medals until Val crutched to the front. Parents, players, and coaches from both teams whooped and cheered her on.

"Yeah, Val!" Makena shouted above the rest.

Mr. Hardin quieted the crowd with his hands.

"Now, the Montreal Fury, champions of the Fiftieth Annual Roberts Cup!"

A scream arose from the Fury girls as they piled forward to gather their loot.

"Can we go now?" Makena whispered to her mother. Makena's mom shook her head.

"It's a pleasure to present our most valuable player award," said Mr. Hardin. From behind the table, his assistant picked up the tallest trophy Makena had ever seen. *Wow*, she thought. *That's huge.*

"This year's recipient led her team with six goals for the tournament, including the game-winning goal today. Miss Ava Dubois!"

Makena clapped as Ava stepped forward. *Six goals in one tournament was pretty impressive*, Makena thought. She hadn't scored any. Ava beamed as she passed the trophy among her teammates. "Now, to our final award," the director said.

Makena nudged her mother.

"Shush," her mom said lightly.

Makena's father gave Makena a stern look.

"This last award is the most important we give out. Any girl or boy from any age group is eligible. It's our sportsmanship award, and this year, it goes to a player on one of the U13 teams standing here."

A hush came over all the girls as they smiled and looked at one another. The assistant reached behind the table and struggled, trying to lift something. Finally, after some laughter, she brought out an impressive-looking trophy nearly as large as the MVP award.

The assistant handed the gigantic trophy to Mr. Hardin, who continued, "Being a star off the field is as big a part of soccer as being a star on the field. Some might say it's an even bigger, more important part. You girls were probably not aware, but in every game, the referee takes notes on more than just the score. He or she grades each team's players on their behavior."

There was a murmur among the crowd of parents and coaches. The players looked at one another.

"One girl was recognized by several referees and by me. For displaying compassion for her friends and opponents, respect for the rules of the game, sportsmanship, and leadership on and off the field, this year's award goes to Miss Makena Walsh of the Brookville Breakers. Makena, come on up here. This is for you."

Makena's jaw dropped as her Soccer Sisters cheered and pushed her forward. Val gave her a nudge with her crutch. Her mother kissed her cheek and wiped a tear from her face. Her father leaned forward, beaming. "You're still grounded," he said and winked.

●　●　●

Well, Papa finally got his hot dog. Turned out they had cool restaurants in Canada too. Sacha's Superdogs wasn't a diner, but it did have about ten pages of hot dog toppings to choose from. Even Jessie was biting into a big, fat chili dog.

"Wow, dith is pretty awthome," she tried to say with a mouthful.

Makena nodded. "Yeah, aren't you glad they don't sell salads?"

Makena was thrilled the whole team could come eat together after the last game. She and her family were moving on to Niagara Falls that night, and most of the other families were making a trip of it as well. Her trophy sat in the middle of the table, hard to see with all the hot dog wrappers piling up, but Makena felt its presence. She was proud of the award and still pensive about all that had happened.

Next to the trophy sat Makena's phone. It made a little beep, and she looked to see a text message from Chloe: Did we win?

Makena showed the phone to Val. Chloe's text was followed by images of soccer balls and hearts.

"Did you tell her? Does she know about last night?" Val asked.

"Nope. And nope."

"Let's do a video call with her," Ariana suggested.

"Oh, good idea!"

"Show her all the hot dogs!" Jessie yelled.

Makena got Chloe on the phone and walked her around the restaurant to show her all the different kinds of buns and toppings they had. Val was having a pizza dog, Makena had a taco dog, and Ariana had something called a Greek dog—no one was quite sure what that involved.

"Oh man, that looks so good," Chloe said. "I bet Papa is going to town."

Makena laughed. "Oh yeah, he's on his second Superdog Supreme and could care less about seeing Niagara Falls."

"How's Val's knee?" Chloe asked.

"Here, I'll let you talk to her for a second."

Val grabbed the phone, and the whole team listened in as she shared the update on her knee and then told Chloe about Skylar pulling the fire alarm in the hotel and getting sent home.

"Whoa," Chloe said. "I can't believe she would do something like that. Wait. Actually, I can. I didn't want to say anything, but I was not a fan."

"She got kicked off the team!" Abby shouted into the phone.

"I know you liked her, Makena, but I'm glad she's not a part of the team anymore," Chloe said.

Makena could see Chloe on the screen. "I did like her at first, but she sure showed me that not all soccer players are Soccer Sisters."

The Breakers all nodded in agreement.

"That girl was just out for herself," Val said. "Definitely *not* a Soccer Sister."

"Yeah," Ariana said. "She broke every rule in the book!"

Makena felt down into her sock. She pulled out the paper she'd been carrying there during the entire tournament. Val had started calling their rules the Code. They had worked on it during the drive to the tournament but had only written down the first few:

1) Team first.
2) Don't be a poor sport or loser.
3) Play with each other and don't take the fun out of it.

"What is that?" Kat asked as Makena spread the weathered piece of paper out on the table, using the trophy to hold it flat.

"It's a thing Val and I were working on," Makena said. "I guess it's a code for our team."

"A code?" Sydney asked.

Ariana looked at the paper and asked, "What, like rules to be on the team?"

"Yeah, kind of," Makena answered. "I've been thinking a lot about it. Watching the way Skylar acted just made me think about what it means to be on this team and to be a true Soccer Sister. So, Val and I started writing rules down."

"Do you guys want to write some?" Makena asked, feeling suddenly unsure.

There was a pause as the girls looked at the list. Makena searched her teammates' eyes, scared she had made a mistake. It was Chloe who broke the silence.

"Hey! Make sure you put one about beating the boys!" Chloe yelled through the phone.

"Let me see." Ariana good-naturedly snatched the list from Makena.

"Here, give it to me," Sydney said, "I'll write it. I have the best handwriting."

"You do not have the best handwriting!" Ella yelled.

"OK, but I do have a sparkle marker." She smiled smugly, reached over, grabbed the Code out of Ariana's hands, and started digging in her soccer bag.

After a minute, she said, "Here, how about this one?"

Makena peered at the growing list to see what Sydney had written.

7) Leave it on the field.

Makena smiled. They all knew that meant you played your heart out and left every ounce of your effort on the field.

"Well, we better write one about bringing snacks. Since you always forget, Ella!" Ariana teased, grabbing the paper and pen. As she turned away, she didn't notice Jessie and Makena polishing off the last of her curly fries.

Makena's heart swelled as they bickered, writing the rest of the rules together—rules they already knew by heart. The Soccer Sisters were her true friends, her teammates, her heart. And always would be. No matter what.

After Ariana finished writing the last rule of the Code, she finally noticed she was out of food.

"Hey, Mac! Give me the pen back," Ariana yelled. "I need to add a rule about stealing the goalie's fries!"

Soccer Sisters Team Code

1. Team first.
2. Don't be a poor sport or loser.
3. Play with each other and don't take the fun out of it.
4. Never put someone down if they make a mistake.
5. Practice makes perfect.
6. Never give up on the field or on one another.
7. Leave it on the field.
8. Always do the right thing.
9. Bring snacks on assigned days.
10. Beat the boys at recess soccer.

Book Club Questions
and Activities

1. Why do you think Makena felt so badly during the Breakers' game the morning after her hot tub adventure with Skylar?

2. Why did Makena go along with all of Skylar's lies to her parents? What would you have done?

3. Should the Breakers' coach have reprimanded Skylar more harshly after her unsportsmanlike actions in the first game? What makes someone a bad sport? A good sport?

4. What do you think is the most important lesson Makena learned from her experiences with Skylar?

5. What other rules would you include in the Soccer Sisters Team Code?

6. If this novel were a movie, which character would you want to play and why?

7. Design your own soccer ball for Makena and the rest of the Soccer Sisters to use in their next tournament.

Meet our Soccer Sisters
Ambassador Brandi Chastain!

Brandi Chastain—NCAA, World Cup, and Olympics icon—is best known for her game-winning penalty kick against China in the 1999 FIFA Women's World Cup final. She also played on the team that won the inaugural Women's World Cup in 1991, Olympic gold medals in 1996 and 2004, and the country's first professional women's league championship.

Chastain is currently the coach of the Bellarmine College Preparatory varsity boys' soccer team and was a color commentator on soccer telecasts for NBC and ABC/ESPN. In addition, Chastain is an active advocate for several causes that are important to her, including safe play and the education of concussion injuries, Crohn's disease and awareness of the illness especially in young children, as well as equal rights for women in sports.

Brandi is married to Jerry Smith, who is the women's soccer coach at her alma mater Santa Clara University. She has one son Jaden and is also a volunteer assistant coach at Santa Clara.

Soccer Sisters Organization

Soccer Sisters aims to inspire and connect young girls and women through sports-based stories and experiences.

We are a for-profit social enterprise aimed at reaching sports-oriented young kids and women with inspiring products and experiences that give back. Our first set of products are the Soccer Sisters book series for middle grade children:

Out of Bounds
Caught Offside
One on One

To learn more about Soccer Sisters, please visit our website and our social handles:

soccersisters.com

Instagram @soccersisters.forever

facebook.com/soccersisters

Twitter @soccersisters

Part of being a Soccer Sister is giving back. Here are some great groups that are supporting soccer and girls all over the world. Check it out!

coachesacrosscontinents.org

Coaches Across Continents is a global leader in the sport for social impact movement.

goalsarmenia.org

Girls of Armenia Leadership Soccer (GOALS) empowers girls throughout the communities of Armenia, using soccer as a vehicle for change and opportunity.

oneworldplayproject.com

One World Play Project encourages the power of play all over the world.

ussoccerfoundation.org

US Soccer Foundation helps foster an active and healthy lifestyle, using soccer to cultivate critical life skills that pave the path to a better future.

fifa.com/womens-football/live-your-goals/index.html

FIFA inspires women and girls to play soccer and stay in the game.

goalsforgirls.org

Goals for Girls uses soccer to teach young women life skills on how to be agents of change in their own lives and in their communities.

Soccer Sisters Roster

BROOKVILLE BREAKERS

Makena Walsh

Valentina Flores

Chloe Gordon

Jessie Palise

Skylar Wilson

Ariana Murray

Harper Jones

Sydney Lin

Abby Rosen

Tessa Jordan

Kat Emelin

Ella Devine

Jasmine Manikas

Coach Lily James

Glossary

50/50 ball: When a player from each team tries to win a loose ball (and they each have a 50/50 chance of doing so).

Assist: When a player gets the ball to a second player, who scores as a result of the pass.

Bench: Where the substitutes sit during the game.

Box: The box that is formed when a line is drawn 18 yards out from each goalpost, along the goal line. The lines extend 18 yards into the field of play and are connected with a line that is parallel to the goal line.

Breakaway: When an offensive player is going to goal with the ball and has left all defenders behind. A rare and very exciting event!

Captain: The player or players who have been designated by the coach or team to lead and represent the team during a game. The captain is the only player allowed to speak to the referee. A captain is often given a distinctive arm band.

Caution: When the referee shows a yellow card to a player after a foul. It's a warning or "caution" to calm down and play by the rules. A player given two yellow cards in one game is ejected from the field! You don't want to get yellow cards.

Center circle: A circle with a ten-yard radius, drawn with the center mark as its center.

Clear: A term used by defenders to send the ball rapidly upfield. This term is yelled out by defenders to alert the defender with the ball that she has impending pressure.

Cleats: Shoes worn by soccer players. So called for the studs or cleats on the soles of the shoes that help grip the grass and prevent slipping.

Corner kick: A kick awarded to the attacking team when the ball, having last been touched by the defending team, crosses the goal line and goes out of bounds. The ball is placed in the corner, duh!

Cross: A ball that has been kicked or thrown (from a throw-in) from near the touch line toward the goal.

Crossbar: The structure of the goal that connects the two upright goalposts.

Dead ball situation: Any situation when the ball is put back into play. Sounds creepy, but isn't.

Dive: When a player fakes being fouled and falls to the ground. Unfortunately, it happens all the time.

Dribble: Moving the ball forward with the feet (similar to basketball, but with your feet!).

Far post: The goalpost that is farthest from the ball.

Forward: An offensive player, playing closest to the opponent's goal.

Foul: An offense against an opponent or against the spirit of the game that results in a free kick.

Free kick: A method of restarting play.

Give-and-go: Just what it sounds like: A player passes to a teammate, runs and gets the ball back from the same teammate. You "give" the ball, and then you "go."

Goal: 1. The structure defined by two upright goal posts and one crossbar that is set on the goal line. 2. To score.

Goal kick: A kick awarded to the defensive team after the attacking team has put the ball over the defending team's goal line. Opposite of a corner kick, the ball is placed close to the goal. Duh #2.

Golden goal: The goal in "sudden victory" overtime that wins and ends the game.

Hand ball: When a player, not the goalie, touches the ball with a hand or part of the arm.

Header: Passing, clearing, controlling, or shooting the ball with the head. This has recently been outlawed for younger kids to prevent collisions and concussions.

Juggling: A practice skill when the ball is kept in the air, using any legal part of the body.

Keepaway: A practice game where the object is for one side to retain possession rather than to score goals.

Near post: The goalpost that is nearest to the ball.

Nutmeg: When a player puts the ball through the legs of an opposing player, a player is said to have been "nutmegged" or "megged." Don't let this happen to you!

Offside: A player is called "offside" when she is nearer to her opponent's goal than both the ball and the second last opponent. It's confusing for many parents and sometimes, players and referees!

Own goal: A goal scored by a player into her own team's net. Very sad event.

Penalty kick: A penalty kick or "PK" is when a shot is taken on goal as a result of a foul committed by the defensive team in their penalty area or "box." All players except the goalie and the player taking the kick must be outside the penalty area when the kick is taken. Penalty kicks are also called "PK's" or "penalties" and can also be used to decide a tied championship game. This is a very stressful, yet exciting event.

Penalty mark: Also called the penalty spot. A circular mark 9 inches in diameter made 12 yards out from the center of the goal where the ball is placed when a penalty kick is to be taken.

Red card: A red card is given to a player who has committed a serious foul or series of bad fouls during a game. A coach or even a parent, can also get "red carded" by yelling at the referee or other bad behavior. Anyone who receives a red card must immediately leave the field. A player who receives a red card can also not play in the next game and her team must continue the game down a player.

Shin guards: Protective equipment worn by players to aid in prevention of injuries to the shin.

Shot: An attempt to score into the opponents goal.

Striker: A position name given to a player in a central attacking position.

Throw-in: When the ball is thrown in by the team that did not kick it out of bounds.

Yellow card: A cautionary measure used by the referee to warn a player not to repeat an offense. A second yellow card in a match results in a red card.

Acknowledgments

If you've gotten this far, you've probably learned a thing or two about what it means to be a Soccer Sister. You don't have to be a girl, or a kid, or even know a single thing about the sport. It's about being a friend and a support—and there are so many people who have been either on my team or cheering me from the sidelines that I want to thank.

To my Soccer Sisters starting lineup: thank you for sticking with me and believing in the power of sport and storytelling. Stacey Vollman Warwick, I could not have done any of this without you. Brandi Chastain, you are my hero. Thank you for always being an inspiration and a true friend (and a great cook!). Marian Smith, thank you for the endless online support and great vision. Chrystian Von Schoettler, you are a logo genius and I love everything you create. Makena Ward, thank you for inspiring me and allowing me to use your first name.

The big hitters (I like to call them my strong offense) are Lauren Sharp, Ed Klaris of Klaris IP, and everyone at Kuhn Projects. Lauren, thank you standing behind me and Soccer Sisters from the beginning and finding the series a great home. You might never have played soccer but you are a star in my eyes. Ed, your guidance made it all possible, and I am forever grateful.

Team Sourcebooks: Thank you so much for believing in Soccer Sisters—you define what it means to be a great team and I'm so grateful to be on yours! Annie Berger, thank you for jumping right in and making everything better. You are a joy to work with and a true Soccer Sister! I also want to thank Aubrey Poole for getting behind me from the start. And thanks to the whole Sourcebooks Team including Nicole Komasinski, Elizabeth Boyer, Kate Prosswimmer, Katy Lynch, Shane White, Alex Yeadon, Steve Geck, and many more!

My players: I've had the honor to coach so many talented girls over the years from Eastchester Rec, to Yonkers, to NY Rush, and now Quickstrike Patriots FC. My greatest joy has seen you grow into strong and confident young women and you were more of an inspiration to me then you will ever know. Thank you girls, really.

Away team: Many others have supported this journey

from every part of my life, from former teammates, coaches, friends and family. Dennis Montalbano, thank you for coaching me through life in general. Teya Montalbano, you're only one call away and if every call did cost a dime, we'd both be broke. Thank you and Evan Rich for helping with so many parts of Soccer Sisters. Carl Hiaasen, you are always a great friend and inspiration. Andy Ward and Jenny Rosenstrach, we meet where our loves collide, books, soccer, food and family, the best place to be in my view. To my huge, loving, and extended family all over the world and the country, as always, your support is everything. MaryAnne Gucciardi, Zach Theiler, Victoria Dokken, Harvard Soccer, Don Cupertino, Steve Davis, Joan Oloff, Esther Newberg, Nick Gates and the entire Coaches Across Continents team, NY Surf, Laura Flynn, Susie Petrucelli, Emily Keenan, Nicole Parent, Tim Wheaton, Ray Leone, Chris Hamblin, Mike Calise, Kerry Baldwin, and the one and only Verenice Merino.

I also need to thank the girls of Armenia. You are fighting to get the equal chance to play, and you will. Thank you for reminding me of the pure joy of being on the field together.

Home Team: Diron Jebejian, and our children Lily and William, everything is always for you. Thank you for your support and your patience and for believing in me, I love you with all my heart.

Don't miss the next book in
this great new series:

Caught
Offside

About the Author

Andrea Montalbano is a writer, advocate, coach, and soccer player. She grew up playing soccer in Miami and took that love to Harvard, where she was a cocaptain and a Hall of Famer. She then attended Columbia University's Graduate School of Journalism, kicking off a long career at NBC News as a writer, producer, and supervising producer for NBC News's TODAY program. Andrea left broadcast journalism to write books and authored *Breakaway* in 2010. Determined to create a series for girls, she spent the next few years writing the three Soccer Sisters novels. Off the field, Andrea is an activist for using sports for social change and has represented the U.S. government abroad to teach the importance of sports for girls. She is a founder of the Girls of Armenia Leadership Soccer charity and is also on several boards for Coaches Across Continents, a global leader in education through sports. She has enjoyed coaching her own two children on local club teams and lives with them and her husband, Diron Jebejian, outside New York City.